Also by Frank Cottrell-Boyce

Millions
Framed
Cosmic
The Astounding Broccoli Boy
Sputnik's Guide to Life on Earth
The Great Rocket Robbery (World Book Day 2019)
Runaway Robot
Noah's Gold

Chitty Chitty Bang Bang Flies Again
Chitty Chitty Bang Bang and the Race Against Time
Chitty Chitty Bang Bang Over the Moon

FRANK
COTTRELL-BOYCE

Illustrated by Steven Lenton

MACMILLAN CHILDREN'S BOOKS

Published 2023 by Macmillan Children's Books
an imprint of Pan Macmillan
The Smithson, 6 Briset Street, London EC1M 5NR
EU representative: Macmillan Publishers Ireland Ltd, 1st Floor,
The Liffey Trust Centre, 117–126 Sheriff Street Upper
Dublin 1, D01 YC43
Associated companies throughout the world
www.panmacmillan.com

Hardback ISBN 978-1-5290-4830-8
Trade paperback ISBN 978-1-0350-1420-0

1 3 5 7 9 8 6 4 2

A CIP catalogue record for this book is available from the British Library.

Printed and bound by CPI Group (UK) Ltd, Croydon CR0 4YY

To Mr Patrick Roose – a magical boy.

For the attention of Las Vegas Metropolitan Police Department: Blackpool, Lancashire, England, UK.

RE OPERATION TOWER: We'd welcome your co-operation.

Last Wednesday, eleven year old girl – name Middy McNulty – told her father she was going out to play with her two cousins Nathan Wiley and Brodie Panatar. Also a large rabbit.

    Her father said, 'OK. But don't go far. Your tea's nearly ready.'

    The children said 'OK.'

    It seems they then went to Las Vegas, Nevada, USA.

Lancashire Constabulary

THE MAGIC CODE

1. NEVER tell anyone how you do your tricks.

2. NEVER do a trick in public until you've learned to do it perfectly. If you do a trick badly people will be able to see how you did it and you will therefore be in breach of rule one.

3. NEVER perform a trick without telling your audience it is a trick. Magic is not the same as lying. The point of lying is to deceive. The point of magic is wonder. Magic is honest deceit.

4. NEVER refer to yourself as 'The Great' or 'The Astounding' or 'The Mysterious', unless you are great, astounding and mysterious. That's lying and therefore a breach of rule 3.

5. NEVER be flashy. Magic is not about showing people how clever you are. People do not trust boastful or flashy people. Wonder comes from trust.

6. NEVER let your eyes look where you don't want the audience to look. The audience is always paying attention. Your job is make sure that they are paying attention to the wrong thing. This is called misdirection

and it's the most important part of magic.

7 NEVER forget, if one magician fools another, that is the highest form of magic. And the fooled magician must show respect to the fooler.

8 NEVER EVER EVER promise that you can do a piece of magic if you are not completely sure, sure you can do it. NOT EVER. JUST DON'T. THAT IS THE WORST.

By the way, Rule Eight is totally and utterly true. Trust us. We know.

Because of Rule One, we can't tell you everything.

But Nathan broke Rule Seven.

He broke one of the laws of magic and before we knew it, we were breaking the actual law.

Anyway, now we're going tell you about the greatest disappearance trick in the world, and how we purely vanished into thin air.

This is how the magic happened.

Signed, The Wonder Brothers

P.S. Nathan can get a bit extravagant at times. But you don't have to believe him. You can believe me instead.

Middy

CHAPTER ONE

WE GO TO AMERICA BY MISTAKE

MIDDY:

To be fair, we did come quietly. As soon as we heard the sirens we knew we were in trouble. There were three police cars in the drop-off zone. Police were jumping out, spreading out, looking for us. Brodie said, 'What are we going to do?'

I said, 'You're the oldest. You're supposed to be in charge. You supposed to tell us what to do.'

Nathan said that thing you never want to hear Nathan say. He said 'Leave this to me.' Then he walked straight out of the front door, right up to one of the police cars and knocked on the driver's window.

'Are you the police?' he said.

The man behind the wheel was wearing a police badge. His car had 'Police' written on the side. The siren on its roof was flashing. He said, 'Yes I am the police.'

'Great,' said Nathan, 'Just who we're looking for.

We want to report a robbery. The thief is right here in this hotel. We're going to help you catch him.'

'Son, I know who you are,' said the police officer. 'Get in the car.'

'Shotgun, shotgun,' said Nathan, trying to bags the front passenger seat.

'In the back,' said the officer. 'Don't play wise with me.'

By now me and Brodie were there too. Brodie said 'Excuse me officer, we've come to America by accident. We'd really like to go home now.'

Being honest, so much had happened to us it was

kind of a relief that an actual grown up was taking charge of us. So I just said 'Hi', and climbed in beside the other two.

Nathan said, 'He's right there in that hotel. We'll lead you right to him. You can arrest him and probably get a medal or promotion or something.'

'Thanks,' said the officer, 'but no thanks. I'm running you to the station.'

CHAPTER TWO

AND NOW . . .THE TWO AND ONLY WONDER BROTHERS!

NATHAN:

Captain Jimenez flashed her Las Vegas Metropolitan Police Department badge and said she wanted to record our interview for 'training purposes'. And also just in case we turned out to be a threat to National Security. Middy thought this was a great idea. She said professional magicians often film themselves when training.

I offered to operate the stop start button.

MIDDY:

Captain Jimenez said that we were in trouble. 'You're in trouble,' she said. 'If you want me to help you, you need to give me the Truth and give it me straight.'

Sadly when she said this she was looking at Nathan. He jumped up, threw out his arms and said to the whole room . . .

'Whoever you are . . .
Whatever you are . . .
Get ready to be astonished
Because we are . . .
THE WONDER BROTHERS!!!!!!'

Captain Jimenez rolled her eyes. 'Son,' she said, 'this is a police investigation, not a circus. Just give us the details. No razzmatazz. Just the facts.'

Saying 'no razzmatazz' to our Nathan is like saying 'no swimming' to Mr Nibbles the goldfish. Razzmatazz is how Nathan moves.

Some people can't see colours. Some can't remember their number bonds. Nathan can't see consequences. He does what he feels like doing. His mum says he's complicated. My mum says he 'can be bouncy'. His teachers call him 'a character'. Basically he's mostly OK but can be a bit of a flapjack sometimes.

'If it's details you're after,' he said, 'you've come to the right people. Officer, we've got more details than you could shake your badge at. We've got details about plumbing, stowaways, brushes with death, magic that will make your skin tingle and the most incredible robbery in the history of the world.. I mean where do we even start?'

'Let's start with your names, shall we?'

'We are the two and only Wonder Brothers. We are . . .' He stopped. I'd given him The Look. One thing you learn when you're part of a magic act with someone is how to watch each other really closely. Close enough to tell what the other is thinking. Like mind-reading. Nathan could tell I was thinking, *Nathan. Stop talking.*

So he stopped talking.

Ta-dah!!!

'The Wonder Brothers,' I said, 'is our stage name. Not our real name. We're not really brothers. For one thing, I'm a girl. We're cousins. I'm Middy McNulty and he is Nathan Wiley.'

'And this is Queenie.' That was Brodie interrupting. 'Queenie's a rabbit,' he said, holding Queenie up so that the officer could see her.

The Captain sat up suddenly. '*Are* you sure that's a rabbit?!' she gasped. 'She's the size of a small child.'

'She nearly won the Best Oversized Rabbit prize at the Lancashire show last year. Do you need to know her full name? It's Queen of Tobago.'

'No. I don't need the rabbit's full name. I need to know what three little British kids are doing wandering around Las Vegas, USA, with no adult supervision.'

Nathan said, 'Like I said, we're here to report a

theft. Someone stole something from our town and we're not going home until we've found it.'

She licked her pencil, ready to take notes. 'OK, let's have a description of your stolen property.'

I explained that the stolen property wasn't exactly ours. 'It belongs to our whole town. To the whole world, really.'

'Just describe it.'

'It's tall and thin and mostly metal.'

'How tall?'

'Five hundred and eighteen feet and nine inches.'

Captain Jimenez got halfway writing that down before she looked up and said, 'Five hundred and . . . What are you talking about?'

'We're talking about the World-Famous Blackpool Tower.'

'How,' snarled the officer, 'would anyone steal a tower?'

'Magic,' said Nathan.

Captain Jimenez put down her pencil and gave him a bad look.

Nathan said, 'You don't believe me. Maybe you don't believe in magic. Don't worry, you will by the time we tell you what happened to us.'

CHAPTER THREE

WELCOME TO BLACKPOOL . . .
HOME OF MAGIC!

NATHAN:

Blackpool people will tell you that the Tower is the tallest or the oldest or the most famous Tower in the whole world. I'm going to be completely honest with you now. It's none of those things. The Eiffel Tower in Paris is bigger and more famous. Our Tower isn't the biggest or the most famous. What it is, though, is the Best. No question.

Listen to this. The bottom bit is a circus. The floor of the top storey is made of glass, so when you walk across it, you can look down at the ground five hundred feet below your Summer shoes. You can pretend you're floating in the air. If you dare. It's called the Walk of Faith. Uncle Kevin says that sometimes he goes to the top of the Tower, looks out to sea and pretends he's a careless cloud.

You can see the Tower from miles away. When we're on our way to Middy's house in the summer, the first one to spot it poking up above the trees and rooftops always shouts, 'I can see it!' And then we know we're nearly there.

Everyone famous has been to Blackpool Tower – Lady Gaga, the Beatles, Will Smith, and people from *Coronation Street*. Also every famous magician ever, including Harry 'Handcuff' Houdini; Max 'the Marvel' Malini and Dai Vernon (also known as the Professor). Probably. And if they haven't, they should have done.

Middy's dad – my uncle Kevin – says, 'This earth spins on its axis. An axis is a spindle that goes right through the middle of a planet. The axis of this planet is Blackpool Tower. The World literally revolves around Blackpool Tower.'

Uncle Kevin should know because uncle Kevin is only the chief electrician of Blackpool Tower and Illuminations, that's all. He's literally in charge of one million light bulbs. His father did the job before him. And his father before that. Going right back. Hence us calling him the Illuminator.

Every year when a big celebrity comes for the Big Switch-On, uncle Kevin gets to stand next to them. You feel right proud seeing him up there next to people who've won the Olympics or *Strictly Come Dancing* or whatever.

Every year the lights have a different theme.

One time it was 'Doctor Who and the Daleks'. Another time, 'Spirits of Ancient Egypt'. This year it's 'Under the Sea'. But that's beside the point.

The point is the celebrity switcher-on this year was the Master of Mystery – Perplexion. You know who that is? Well, I mean, no one knows who he is in real life. Because he's a mystery. No one knows where he's from. Or how old he is. Or what language he speaks, because he hardly ever speaks at all. But everyone knows he is the greatest magician in the world.

When Middy's dad told us it was going to be Perplexion, we couldn't even believe him. Why would Perplexion come to Blackpool Tower?

'Because Blackpool is the home of magic and the centre of the world. Also because he's just done a massive farewell tour – Moscow, Rome, Berlin, Paris, London – so . . . why not stop here to turn on the lights before he goes home? That's all he's doing. Turning the lights on.'

I said, 'Is he doing a show? Can we go? Can we MEET HIM?'

'He's not doing a show here. He's doing one big, spectacular last ever show in Las Vegas, and then – no more Perplexion. All the greatest magicians in the worldwill be there. But here in Blackpool. . . he's just switching on the lights. As for meeting him, he doesn't talk to ordinary folk.'

'But he'll talk to you, uncle Kevin – you're the Illuminator. And besides, we're not ordinary folk. We're fellow magicians.'

Uncle Kevin said even he wouldn't be talking to Perplexion directly. 'It's all done through his bodyguard and his glamorous assistant.'

Auntie Anya said, 'Don't call her the glamorous assistant. She's a talented woman. And she has a name. Zenith.' Auntie Anya by the way is the Boss Plumber of Blackpool Tower. She's in charge of like a million gallons of water and miles of piping. That's why we call her Aqua Auntie. 'Besides,' she said, 'Perplexion won't need any assistance. All he's got to do is turn the lights on. And go. But – as long as Brodie doesn't mind looking after you – I might just be able to swing it for you to stand in the wings when he's doing the switch-on.'

Brodie is supposed to be able to look after us because he's, like, one year older. Brodie is not interested in looking after anything except his rabbit.

But standing on the side of the stage would be beyond amazing. We'd be so close to the Master of Mystery.

Brodie said, 'Will there be any bangs or flashes or loud noises or anything that might frighten a rabbit?'

Uncle Kevin said, 'He's literally going to appear, turn the lights on and then disappear.

15

Queenie should be all right.'

Middy thought this was going to be the greatest moment of her life. 'This is going to be the greatest moment of my life,' she said. 'We have got to get to talk to him.'

I reminded her that Perplexion doesn't talk and that magicians are not supposed to tell how they do their tricks.

'But if I show him one that he doesn't know, then he has to show me one that I don't know. That's the rules. That's how good magicians become great magicians. They learn from each other. Imagine having the Master of Mystery as a mentor.'

CHAPTER FOUR

NOW YOU SEE IT,
NOW YOU DON'T . . .

NATHAN:

I know he said he wasn't going to do a magic show, but when Perplexion appears, well, just his appearance is magic. Absolutely the whole town was crowding around the stage waiting for Perplexion to appear and turn the lights on.

First of all, his bodyguard came onto the stage. He was wearing a suit and little pair of round, very dark sunglasses that made it look like he had holes instead of eyes and a skull instead of a face. But a skull with ginger hair. Why anyone needs sunglasses at all after the sun has gone down, I don't know. Anyway, he inspected the stage for anything that might injure or annoy Perplexion, while uncle Kevin checked all the electrics.

Ever since the Tower was built the person in charge of the lights gets to introduce the person who is going to switch them on. So uncle Kevin tapped the microphone a few times, then said, 'Blackpool, are you ready to welcome

. . . the Master of Mystery himself . . . Perplexion!'

Massive roar from everyone. Especially us. The bodyguard moved to the side of the stage and looked down into the audience, watching for trouble. The curtains at the back swished open and out came . . . not Perplexion. But Zenith. She was so glamorous. She didn't say anything, just stood in the shadows with her hands clasped in front of her as though she was holding something really fragile. Like a baby bird, maybe.

She looked down and opened her fingers just a bit. You could see there was something glowing and flickering in her hands. It splashed a bit of light onto her face. Everyone was trying to figure out what it could be. Was she carrying a hot coal in her hand or something?

She opened her fingers wider. The little light whooshed up out of her hands towards the top of the Tower like a luminous bird. Everyone craned their necks, trying to see what it would do. When it was almost out of sight, it burst like a firework rocket. But when a firework rocket bursts into sparks, it disappears. This seemed to hover over the very top of the Tower like a really small planet.

Then it started slowly, slowly floating down.

The whole town was silent. You've never heard quiet as quiet as that. Every eye, every brain was focused on that strange glowy, floaty shape as it got nearer and nearer to us.

'Anticipation,' whispered Middy, 'that's what this is. Everyone holding their breath waiting to see what will happen. Karabas says *Anticipation is the first course in the feast of magic*. Literally page one of her book, *My Secrets Revealed*.'

She's always quoting that book. I was just concentrating on this light. I couldn't look away. Neither could anyone else. As it got nearer, you could see it was the shape of a man. A bit nearer, and you could see that the man had sticky-up hair. He was looking down at us.

It couldn't be, could it?

It couldn't be that Perplexion was floating down from the top of the five-hundred-foot Tower?

It looked like him, but you could see right through him to the girders and the staircases of the Tower. As if Perplexion was some kind of golden ghost.

Down on the stage, Zenith was standing with her back to us, staring up at floaty-ghost Perplexion just like everyone else.

The golden ghost seemed to put its arms around Zenith, then turn her round to face us and then – this bit was proper magic – there was a flash of light. And where Zenith had been standing there was Perplexion. Just like that! Wearing a pair of shiny silver trousers. It was definitely him. I mean it couldn't be anyone else. Who else is nearly seven-foot-tall, skinny as a stick

19

of rock, with a plume of moon-
blonde hair sticking straight up
on top of his head, making
him look even taller?

Everyone was like,
how in all glory did
that happen?

Where <u>did</u>
Zenith go? And
then he pointed
towards the back of
the crowd, to where
the sea was washing up
against the promenade –
standing on the roof of
one of those funny-looking
storm shelters, her red dress
flapping in the breeze, was Zenith.

One minute she was in front of
us.

Then she was behind us.

We never saw her move an inch.

At this point hardly anyone was
even breathing, they're so amazed.

If that's
not Wonder
Time, what
is?!!!

And he hadn't
even turned
the Illuminations
on yet!

Middy whispered
again, 'It's called
misdirection. While we
were all looking up at the
ghost thing, he could have
marched a herd of elephants
across that stage and none
of us would've noticed.'

I shushed her. 'This is
your dad's big moment,' I said.

Her dad – the Illuminator –
asked Perplexion to come forward
and pull the lever that switches
the lights on. Perplexion shook his
head. He's not going to pull the
lever. He points a finger at the
lever. And the lever pulls itself!!!

We all watch it moving slowly,
slowly into position. Then . . .

Bang!

The lights are on.

And Blackpool Illuminations have started.

A river of coloured lights flooded the promenade. A massive red octopus dangled its tentacles over our heads. A giant silver squid shot up and down the promenade, squirting clouds of starfish out of its bum. Flashing crabs snapped their claws on top of every lamp-post. And just in front of the pier, a huge King Neptune was waving a neon trident. After a while everything went blue and everyone went 'Oooh!!' because now we were standing under a mile-long whale. It lifted its tail, blew a fountain of flickers, then sank into the dark.

Rising high above all the other lights, like a firework on top of a cake, was Blackpool Tower itself. As soon as the whale disappeared, the lights on the Tower arranged themselves into the shape of a big, red beating neon heart, as if the Tower was saying *I Love You* to us all.

Everyone smiled up at that beating heart.

You know the way that there was one current of electricity flowing through all those million light bulbs, lighting them up, joining them together? Well, just then there was one current of Wonder flowing through all the people on the

22

prom. And in the light of that beating heart, all their faces shone like different-coloured light bulbs. That's when a crowd turns into an audience.

Middy said, 'My dad did that.'

Then all the lights went out.

I don't just mean the *Lights*.

I mean every light along the front – the lights on the Tower, the lights of the little kiosks that sell sticks of rock, sweets and silly hats, the lights on the tram stop, the streetlights.

All of them.

The Tower's big red heart carried on beating for a few seconds. Then stopped as though someone had unplugged the whole town. It felt like someone had dropped a big black duvet over everything.

At first there were voices all around – mostly mums and dads saying things like, 'Where are you?' And, 'Don't let go of my hand.' I could hear Brodie saying, 'Don't be scared, don't be scared,' to Queenie. I was going to explain to him that rabbits are not afraid of the dark because rabbits live underground, but I didn't get the chance. Everything and everyone suddenly went quiet because . . . well, because amazement.

There are some things you can see in the dark that you could never see in the light.

A huge, heavy yellow moon. A glitterball of stars dangling from the sky. Waves that sparkled in the moonlight as they rushed and crashed onto the beach. It made you want to dash down and dive in.

'This,' said Middy, 'is the best trick ever.'

I knew what she meant. Standing there, under the stars, with the sound of the waves – it was like all of ordinary life was misdirection. That the real magic was there all around us all the time. We were just too busy to see it.

Middy said, 'He did this on purpose.'

'Who did?'

'Perplexion.' But as soon as she said that, she started to look worried. She looked behind her – at the stage. I knew what she was thinking. Of course I did. When you're in a magic act with someone, you have to watch them so closely that after a while you can always tell exactly what they're thinking. Middy was worrying that if something had gone wrong with the lights, maybe it was her dad's fault.

Then – *Bang!* – the lights all came back on again and everyone cheered.

'Yeah,' said Middy. 'They definitely did that on purpose.' She looked at the stage again and there, standing in the spotlight, was . . . nothing.

Perplexion had vanished.

I looked back – and Zenith had disappeared too.

It's like Middy said: misdirection. You make the audience look one way – up at the stars or at a golden ghost – but meanwhile all the magic is happening somewhere else.

Except it wasn't just Zenith and Perplexion who had vanished.

Middy was the first to notice.

'The Tower!' she gasped. 'The Tower is gone!'

Until then, everyone was thinking their own thoughts. Thoughts like, *Aren't stars amazing?* Then, in a flash, everyone was thinking the same thought. As though the whole of Blackpool was one giant brain and every person was one cell in that brain and that whole brain was staring at . . . nothing.

Because where there should have been a world-famous five-hundred-foot, one-hundred-and-fifty-year-old tower with a heart of red neon, there was . . . nothing.

Blackpool Tower had vanished.

'Tower's gone then,' said Brodie.

'The Tower has gone!' I said.

'I just said that,' said Brodie.

'At least I said it with an exclamation mark! If you'd said it with an exclamation mark, we'd have been prepared.'

'Not sure,' said Brodie, 'how a whole tower can just disappear though.'

'It's probably just a fuse,' said Middy. She thinks she's an electricity expert just because her dad's the Illuminator.

But I knew the real answer.

The answer was magic.

CHAPTER FIVE

THE BIGGEST VANISHING
TRICK OF ALL TIME

CAPTAIN JIMENEZ:

It seemed somewhat surprising that a five-hundred-foot feat of Victorian engineering could disappear in the flash of a light bulb. I did suggest they might be messing with my meatloaf. The girl, Middy, responded with a lecture on the hows and whys and history of large objects disappearing. I will admit she seems knowledgeable about this subject.

MIDDY:

Magicians have vanished big things before. For instance during a posh dinner in London once, David Berglas made a grand piano disappear while someone was playing it. David Copperfield made a jumbo jet vanish. Which sounds amazing until you find out that he also made the Statue of Liberty vanish.

Let's get one thing straight before we go any further.

When I say 'magicians', I'm not talking about some kind of wand-wavy people who say a few spells and turn their enemies into cheesecake. I'm talking about proper magic – rabbits out of hats, card tricks, people levitating and things vanishing. Magic that you have to work at.

To do a real magic trick, you have to spend ages making it look like something impossible happened. If impossible things really happened, they wouldn't be impossible. If something that seems to be impossible happens – like Blackpool Tower disappearing – that's because you don't know what made it possible.

Real magicians – including me and Nathan – won't tell you how they did it because it's against the rules to tell how you did a trick. But we will tell you that it wasn't *magic* magic. It was hard work, cleverness and crazy amounts of preparation.

I knew right away when the Tower disappeared that it wasn't *magic* magic; it was magic. Like Wonder Brothers magic. Only bigger. I couldn't tell how you how it was done, but all the signs were there. It happened at night, for one thing, when you can't see that well anyway. Then there was the business with all the lights going out. That felt like a piece of what we magicians call 'misdirection'. That's when you make the audience pay attention to the wrong thing so that you can do the magic bit without them noticing. Turning off all the lights in town and making everyone look up at the wonders of the universe – that's classic misdirection.

Everyone rushed over to look at the place where the Tower used to be. When we got there, security guards were putting barriers around the whole site and telling everyone to keep back. Someone said they had to do that because it was a crime scene now. Someone had stolen the Tower. Someone else said it was in case of radioactivity because it looked like the Tower had been vaporised. I explained to Nathan that the vanishing was a magic trick. But Nathan was more interested in Brodie's explanation. Brodie's explanation was, 'The Tower has shrunk.'

'Brodie, metal doesn't shrink.'

'It doesn't vanish either. And if it really didn't shrink, what's that?'

In the space on the prom where the Tower normally stood, was a four-foot model, correct in every detail.

Nathan got excited about that. 'What if . . .' he said,

'whoever did it is going to shrink something else? Like the pier? Or the Big One!' The Big One is the tallest rollercoaster in the UK. 'Imagine if it ended up as the smallest. Oh. Wait. What about the people who were on the tower? Have they shrunk?'

'That,' I said, 'is not a shrunken Tower. That is the original architect's model. It's been on display in the reception area since the centenary celebrations in 1994. It has not changed size.'

Everyone in the crowd had a different answer to how the Tower had vanished. And every answer was as crazy as Brodie's. Stuff like, 'Really ambitious thieves . . . You can get good money for scrap metal.' And, 'Aliens or the town council. They're as bad as each other.'

I said, 'This is a disappearing trick. Like when David Copperfield disappeared the Statue of Liberty. Or David Berglas disappeared that piano.'

Brodie pointed out that Blackpool Tower is bigger than a piano. A lot bigger.

'Is it bigger than the Statue of Liberty though?'

I said, 'Yes it is. The Tower is bigger. So this is the biggest vanishing trick of all time. And it's happening here. In our town. This is cracking stuff. This is a magic trick. By Perplexion!'

We'd always, always wanted to see Perplexion doing magic. When I saw he'd vanished from the stage, I had a wave of sadness, thinking – that's it. No more Perplexion. He's going to do one more show, on the other side of the world. We'll never see him now except on YouTube or whatever. We'll never find out how he did his magic.

And now, he'd done the biggest trick of his life right here in our town, right in front of our eyes. Well, right behind our backs. It was a thrill.

'Not sure,' said Brodie. Brodie is never sure. If you asked Brodie if his pants were on fire, he'd say he wasn't sure. 'The bit I like best about a vanishing trick,' he said, 'is when the vanished thing comes back. Is the Tower going to come back?'

'He's right,' said Nathan. 'Vanishing something isn't magic. Things vanish all the time. They get lost. They fade away. The magic part of a vanishing trick is when the thing un-vanishes. Look it up in your book.'

I've got a little book that I take with me everywhere. I've got it here now. It's by Karabas the Modest (Second-Best Magician of All Time) and it's called *My Secrets Revealed*. It tells you the Karabas Rules, including the rule about not revealing the secrets of your tricks. Which is a pretty confusing thing to find in a book that is actually CALLED *My Secrets Revealed*.

To be fair, magicians only tell you the basics of how they do their tricks. You have to work most of it out for yourself. Or invent a trick that is so good that other magicians will want to swap magic with you.

Anyway, I looked in *My Secrets Revealed* and on page fifty six she says this about vanishing things:

> *In a vanishing trick you make something that the volunteer really loves – their wedding ring, or their best friend – disappear. And when they reappear the volunteer is filled with the happiness that comes from remembering that you really love something. The really magic thing that appears at the end of a vanishing trick is not the wedding ring or the car keys or even the Statue of Liberty. It's hope. Or love.*

I've actually underlined that bit.

Great magicians un-vanish things in surprising ways. Harry Kellar, for instance, used to take a wedding ring from someone in the audience, put it in a gun, fire the gun into a box, open the box and – *Ta-dah!* There was your wedding ring on a ribbon TIED ROUND THE NECK OF A HAMSTER.

When I explained this to Nathan he said, 'So you think that any minute now, Blackpool Tower is going to reappear, tied to the neck of a hamster.'

'That does sound good actually,' said Brodie.

'I'm not saying anything about hamsters. I'm saying

that the Tower is going to come back, and when it does, it's going to be . . . I can't even think of a word to say how cracking it's going to be. We're never going to forget this moment.'

So we stood there holding our breath waiting for this unforgettable moment to come.

People began to drift away, to the hot-dog stands, and the candyfloss sellers, and the trams that trundled up and down the Illuminations.

Brodie said 'Queenie's getting cold. I'm going to take her home.'

Brodie is supposed to be in charge of us, so if he goes, we all have to go. I pleaded with him. I said, 'Brodie, we can't go now. History could be coming here any minute now.'

But he went and we had to go with him.

I walked backwards nearly the whole length of the prom, keeping my eye on the spot where history might happen.

But it didn't.

CHAPTER SIX

ATTENTION!

NATHAN:

First thing next morning, I got up before anyone else, pulled down the loft ladder and crept up it. Middy's house has got a window in the roof. You can always see the Tower from up there. Well, you can see the Tower from nearly everywhere. But I really like sticking my head out of the loft window. Also, that loft is where Middy showed me my first magic trick.

It turned out I wasn't the first up. Middy was already up there, her head sticking out of the window. 'It's still vanished,' she said.

I squeezed in next to her. There was the Tower, still gone. At the end of the road, between the trees, there was a great big Nothing reaching from behind the roof of St Cuthbert's right up into the sky.

We went back downstairs. In the kitchen, Middy's dad was scrolling through his phone.

Middy said, 'It's still missing.'

He said, 'What is?' without looking up from his phone.

'The Tower.'

'Oh that.'

I said, 'Is anyone going to do anything about it?'

'Middy,' he said, ignoring me, 'I have literally got one million light bulbs to look after. Not to mention plugs and fuses. So if anyone is going to do something about it, it won't be me, OK?'

Fair enough. That's why we call him the Illuminator.

I mentioned the disappearance to Auntie Anya.

'Are you sure?' she said. She was on her phone too. 'Maybe it's the weather. You know sometimes you can see the mountains across the bay, and sometimes you can't. This is the seaside. The view is always changing. Remember the time we climbed Pendle Hill and we were halfway up it before we saw it.'

'Yeah, but—'

'Middy, I'm really busy. If you're so bothered, go and check.'

How could she be busy, by the way? How busy can you be if your job is head plumber of a building that isn't there any more?

'OK,' said Middy, 'Can we go down and check?'

'Only if Brodie is happy to go with you and keep an eye on things,' added her mum.

So Brodie took us down to the prom to make sure

that Blackpool Tower was still missing.

And, it was.

There were a lot of other people there already. Standing around with their hands in their pockets as if waiting for a five-hundred-foot tower to reappear was just like waiting for a bus. One was holding up a postcard of the Tower as if we might have forgotten what it looked like. A woman with a very loud voice was telling her mate that she'd never been up the Tower. 'Lived here all my life and never thought to go up. When you think something's always going to be there, you just don't get round to it,' she said.

A man in a bright blue coat was weaving in and out of the crowd, selling silver souvenir models of the Tower from a box. Right at the top of the sky, a plane was drawing a line of smoke across the blue. I noticed Middy looking up at it. I notice everything she does, and she notices everything I do. It's a magic-act thing.

'I just remembered,' she said, 'Dad said Perplexion was flying out first thing this morning. Maybe he's already gone. He can't un-vanish the Tower if he's not here.'

'We should do some magic to cheer them up. That's what magic is for,' said Brodie.

I don't know where that 'we' came from. The Wonder Brothers is me and Middy. Brodie is just a big cousin with a big rabbit and a mission to look after us.

Anyway, I got the magic going.

Whoever you are . . .
Whatever you are . . .
Get ready to be astonished
Because we are . . .
THE WONDER BROTHERS!

I did an attention grabber. That's a trick that's meant to grab the crowd's attention. Our attention-grabber is dead simple. We clap our hands and clouds of blue smoke appear. It's not a proper magic trick. Anyone can do it. You just buy a packet of special blue smoke powder from Maggie's Marvellous Magic Mart (Est. 1922). It's actually called Attention! Any trick that you can buy in a packet is called a gimmick.

But it does grab people's attention. Everyone is looking in the same place and you can feel that current, connecting everyone up like the million light bulbs in the Illuminations.

So we did our trick. It's called Rock and Roll. It's not a gimmick. It's a proper trick, invented by Middy. She calls it Rock and Roll because it involves a stick of Blackpool rock and a bread roll. It goes like this . . .

Middy pulls a bread roll out of her backpack. Then she asks the crowd if anyone has a stick of Blackpool Rock. I mean it's Blackpool, so that's definitely going to be a yes. The trick is, Middy takes the Blackpool rock, asks the kid their name, then she puts the stick of rock inside a bread roll (hence why the trick is called Rock and Roll – one stick of rock and a bread roll). Then I ask the kid to take a bite out of the rock and the roll. And when the rock is broken, instead of having *Blackpool* written down the middle, it has the kid's own name.

Wonder Time!

It's a cracker of a trick. Everyone loves it. Even the TV crew who were there from the news came over to look. And that's when I said that thing about we promise to bring the Tower back to Blackpool.

CAPTAIN JIMENEZ:

'Excuse me, you said what?'

CHAPTER SEVEN

ROCK AND ROLL

MIDDY:

First of all, it didn't happen like that.

For one thing, the trick did not go well.

Nathan did the attention grabber. That worked. It always works. It got everyone's attention, including the attention of the TV people who were filming the Vanishing Tower for the news. They were having a tough morning. I mean, how do you film something that isn't there any more?

They were probably right relieved to see two little kids doing a magic act. The reporter had a bright yellow suit and hair that didn't move, even in the seaside wind. She pointed her microphone at me – not Nathan – and asked me what we were going to do. I said we were the Wonder Brothers and we were going to do a trick called Rock and Roll.

'Why's it called Rock and Roll?'

'Wait and see,' I said.

I can't tell you how the trick is done, but I will admit it only works if the kid is called Olivia, Harry, Mohammed, Jack, Ava, Freddy, Maryam, Leo or Sophie.

We found a Freddy in a yellow hat shaped like a duck. I asked him where he got his hat.

'Won it.'

I said, 'Where did you win that hat, Freddy?' You have to keep asking the kid their name so that the audience remembers it.

'I won it in PleasureLand. I hooked ten ducks.'

'Did you win that stick of rock too, Freddy?'

'No. Bought it.'

'What does the writing in the rock say, Freddy?' See? We've said 'Freddy' three times now. Subtle skills.

'It says *Blackpool*. It's Blackpool rock.'

'Let me see.'

Nathan held up the stick of rock for everyone to see, then placed it inside the bread roll. The news camera zoomed in on the rock while the kid took a bite.

'Now, Freddy,' – fourth time we'd said his name – 'take a look at your stick of Blackpool rock, Freddy. What does the writing in the middle say now?'

Freddy slowly looked up from the rock. He looked at me. He looked at Nathan. Then he looked at his mum. Then he burst into tears.

'This –' he sniffed – 'is not my rock.'

Nathan said, yes it WAS his stick of rock, but something magical had happened to change it. 'What's changed, Freddy?'

'It's not my rock.' Freddy sniffed.

The camera went right in on the rock. So the whole nation could see that it said FREDDY now. Surely the nation must have been impressed. The TV reporter definitely was. 'Whoah!' she said. 'Incredible! What do you think of that, Freddy?' She put her microphone up to Freddy's mouth. The camera zoomed in on Freddy's face and Freddy burst into tears. 'IT'S NOT MY ROCK,' he wailed. 'My rock says *Blackpool* in the middle.'

Nathan said, 'And what is written in it now?' Just to clarify that the trick had worked, even if Freddy didn't like it.

'This is not my rock. I don't want this.'

The newswoman said, 'It IS your rock. But now instead of *Blackpool*, it says *Freddy*—'

'I WANT MY ROCK BACK!!!'

The reporter looked at me and said, 'Maybe you should give him his rock back?'

'It IS his rock. I've upgraded it. By magic. See . . . your name, so . . . your rock.' I looked into the camera and said '*Ta-dah*!'

Normally '*Ta-dah!*' gets you a round of applause. All I got was the reporter with the immobilized hair staring at me as though I'd just eaten poor little Freddy's rock right in his face. And now Freddy's mum got in on the act.

'Just,' she snarled, 'give him back his rock.'

Other people were filming us now, not just the news crew. Flocks of phones were glowing around us, accusingly.

The reporter said to the cameraman 'We should move on.'

I was wishing the ground would open up and swallow me. It seemed like the right moment to vanish ourselves quietly into the crowd. But Nathan isn't one to do things quietly. When it's time to leave quietly, he'll always go loud. He stood between me and the cameras and – that's when he said it.

'Wipe away your tears!' he said – honestly I don't know where he gets it from. 'Wipe away your tears because the Wonder Brothers are here, to make you happy and to fill your hearts with wonder.'

'If you want to make people happy,' snarled Freddy's mum, 'try leaving their sweets alone.'

'Exactly!' said Nathan. 'No more confectionary magic! We are going to . . .' Nathan looked straight into the camera. 'For our next trick,' he said, 'we will bring back Blackpool Tower!'

Everyone gasped. Some people started clapping. The reporter in the yellow suit waded through the crowd to get near him. I grabbed him by the elbow and pushed him towards the tram stop.

'What did you say that for?' I hissed. 'You've just promised everyone something impossible.'

'But that's what magic is. You promise to do something impossible, and then you do it.'

'Nathan. Magicians know how they're going to do it before they say they're going to do it.'

'You'll work it out. You always do.'

NATHAN:

What Middy hasn't told you, Captain, is that we are definitely going to get that Tower back.

I know because the night it disappeared I had a dream.

In the dream we were on-stage in Las Vegas. A great big stage. Thousands of people were watching us. And there, in the front row, you could see more famous magicians than you could shake a wand at. There was David Copperfield and David Blaine, Dynamo and Dorothy Dietrich, Fay Presto, Chris Ramsay and Chris Pilsworth. And obviously Perplexion. They were all watching us and they were awestruck because we were doing this beautiful trick that none of them had seen before.

Then I stepped forward and said, '*Whoever you are . . . Whatever you are . . . Get ready for Wonder because, for our next trick, we are going to . . .*' And then I woke up.

When I described the dream, the only reaction was the sound of Queenie chewing slowly on her carrot.

Captain Jimenez said, 'And your point is?'

'My point is, in the dream, we were half a world away from home. In Las Vegas. And now, here we are, half a world away from home. In Las Vegas.'

I mean to say. Trust the dream.

CHAPTER EIGHT

THE ELEPHANT IN THE ROOM

CAPTAIN JIMENEZ:

At this point, Sergeant Jamie arrived with my doughnut and coffee. The boy Brodie asked if there was any chance of tea and biscuits. He was very specific about the biscuits (chocolate digestive). He also requested carrots for his rabbit.

I explained that this was a police interview, not an English tea party.

The boy Brodie replied, 'We are quite hungry though.'

I said that the sooner they told me the facts, the sooner they could eat. 'So far what I've got is that you are accusing someone of stealing a large building. And you came to Las Vegas because of a dream?'

The other boy, Nathan, said – quote – 'What's unusual about that? Everyone in Las Vegas is here because of a dream. It's on all the posters. It's painted on the side of the buses. *Follow your Dream.*

Live the Dream. Dream the Dream. It's everywhere. What makes us unusual?'

I pointed out that in those sentences, 'dream' means something like ambition. It does not refer to literal dreams. 'If I followed my actual dreams,' I said, 'I would be sitting here in my pyjamas. Because that's the dream I mostly have. That I turn up to work having somehow forgotten to get dressed.'

The boy Brodie said he often had the same dream about school.

The girl Middy, concurred.

I pointed out that this only proved my point. I turned to Sergeant Jamie. 'Now on the one hand, Sergeant,' I said, 'I've got to deal with three kids and a rabbit who shouldn't even be in the country. That's one pile of paperwork. On the other hand, I've got a whole list here of crimes and misdemeanours. That's another pile of paperwork. Then when I try to get some sense out of these children, they shower me with moonshine and baloney about dreams and disappearing buildings.'

In response to this, Sergeant Jamie said, 'Ma'am, maybe you should take a look this.' He showed me something on YouTube that showed the seafront of Blackpool, England. 'It does seem, ma'am, as though there's no Tower there.'

'Sergeant,' I said, 'there's no elephant in this room.

That doesn't mean there was an elephant in the room earlier.'

'Yes, ma'am.'

'And the fact that there's no big Tower in Blackport . . .'

'Blackpool, Ma'am.'

'. . . does not mean that there used to be.'

But further investigation revealed that there really did used to be a fine looking Tower there and the people were real fond of it. There were clips on YouTube of people saying how it was a Wonder of the world how they'd climbed that Tower as children every summer, or gone there on their first date with the love of their life. One guy talked about how his mother had asked to go to the very top when she was not long for this Earth. She said it made her feel like she was already halfway to Heaven.

Behind them all was the empty space their big, beloved Tower used to be.

'It just vanished,' one of them said, 'right in front of our very eyes.'

CHAPTER NINE

HEY PRESTO!

MIDDY:

OK, maybe we've been telling you this story in the wrong order. On page seventeen of *My Secrets Revealed*, Karabas the Modest (Second-Best Magician of All Time) says the most important thing in magic is doing things in the right order. Like if you show the audience a hat with a rabbit inside, that's unusual, but it's not surprising. If you first show them an empty hat, *then* take a rabbit out of that empty hat, *that* is surprising.

Empty hat.

Hat with rabbit inside.

That's the right order.

That's magic.

I think it's probably the same with telling the truth.

We should have started by explaining about me and Nathan and magic. Because the actual real answer to, 'How did three little kids from England end up in Las

Vegas, Nevada with no adults?' is . . . Nathan.

This is exactly the kind of thing that happens when you hang out with Nathan.

This is how Dad describes Nathan . . .

'If you drop a Mento into a bottle of Coke and stand right back, the bottle erupts. A spinning volcano of Coke sprays bubbles all over the garden. You might end up laughing or you might end up with a bottle top in your eye. All because of that Mento. Well that Mento is Nathan.'

I don't have any brothers or sisters, but every year most of my cousins come to stay at ours for the summer. Because . . . well, we live in Blackpool. So who wouldn't want to come and stay? Also we have a garden. I have some cracking older cousins – such as Big Bindi and Nice Charlie. I also have cousins like Brodie and Nathan.

Not going to lie, Nathan can be fun. Like the time Charlie and Bindi got aggy and starting shoving each other around. Nathan said, 'Cousins! I have a sensational notion! A sensational, sensational notion.' The notion was to turn this scrap into a wrestling tournament with rules and proper Wrestling Names.

I was Mad Middy, Bindi was the Bad B, Charlie was Johnny Crush. Brodie isn't so fond of wrestling, so he was the referee. He's not an ideal referee. Ask him about rabbits, he will talk for a week. Ask him anything else, he will just shrug 'not sure'. 'Not sure' is not the best attitude for a referee. Also any referee who won't let go of his rabbit lacks authority.

Anyway, this is how the Wonder Brothers began.

A couple of Summers ago, we were in the middle of a game of Den-O when Nathan vanished. Completely. Den-O is just hide-and-seek. So you are supposed to vanish. But not completely. We seeked Nathan for so long we began to forget what he looked like. We seeked and seeked and nothing. First we were impressed, then we were bored, then we were worried.

I asked Dad if he'd seen Nathan. Dad said, 'Who?'

'Nathan. Our Nathan. My cousin Nathan. He's staying here for the summer. He stays here every Summer. Nathan, your brother's son.'

'I know who Nathan is. What about him? I'm on the phone.'

He was on the phone, to be fair – but then, when isn't he on the phone?

'We can't find him.'

'I'm sure he'll turn up.'

'He's not a set of car keys, Dad. He's a missing kid.'

I asked Brodie.

'Not sure,' he said. 'There's a kid on your roof. Could that be him?'

And there was Nathan, perched on the pointy top of the roof. One leg dangling towards the back garden, and one towards the front, like a cowboy, but a cowboy riding a three-storey house instead of a horse.

We shouted up to him, pleading with him to come back down.

'How?' he shouted.

'How did you get up there?'

'Don't remember.'

Then he made it clear that he would welcome any advice on how to get down by yelling, 'Help! Get me down!' at the top of his voice until finally Dad came out into our garden and the neighbours came out into theirs.

The man in number eight had an extra-tall ladder because he did window cleaning. He lent us the big ladder, but he wouldn't go up it – he said he didn't want to be responsible.

'I could hold it,' he said, 'while one of you go up.'

Quite a lot of people volunteered to hold the ladder. No one at all volunteered to go up it. Meanwhile Nathan kept shouting that he was falling, which he really wasn't, by the way. But he kept shouting it until, in the end, Dad got Nice Charlie to hold the ladder while he shimmied up it to rescue Nathan.

'Is your dad Santa Claus?' asked Big Bindi. 'Because he can't half walk on roofs.'

Maybe Dad IS Santa. But it wasn't him who got Nathan down off the roof.

It was me.

In all the faff, everyone seemed to have forgotten something. There's a window in our roof. I dashed inside and ran upstairs. Sure enough on the landing the hatch that led to the loft was open and the ladder we always used to get up there was in place. I climbed up.

The loft was still cluttered full of boxes of stuff we hadn't got round to unpacking from when we moved in. When we put our boxes in the loft, there were still boxes up there from when the last people moved in.

There's probably boxes up there from when the very first owners lived there back in Victorian times or whatever.

Nathan had put two of these boxes on top of each other and climbed out. I stood on tip-toe and looked out. There was one of his feet dangling just a few feet above my head.

'Nathan,' I hissed. 'Nathan.'

'What?' He didn't look down. He said, 'You can see Blackpool Tower from up here.'

I said, 'You can see Blackpool Tower from everywhere. You can see it five towns away. You can see it from across the sea. Get down and come in, you massive doughnut.'

'Can't.' He was still staring at the Tower where it stuck up above the roofs of the houses opposite. He couldn't look down.

'Lean forward, hold on and swing your other leg back over.'

'What if I slip?'

'I can nearly reach you. If you lie down and hold on, I can pull you in.'

'I can't look.'

His whole brain was on pause. He was stuck, staring straight ahead.

I said, 'Do you want to see me suck a whole pencil up my nose and into my head?'

Who is not going to look when you say a thing like that?

Nathan looked down. I held up a pencil and then I did this little magic trick that Dad had shown me ages ago. You're not supposed to tell anyone how to do magic tricks. It's one of the sacred rules of magic. So I can't go into details here. Maybe later. But it's this really simple trick where you stick just the tip of a pencil up your nose and then you pretend to sniff the whole pencil. The pencil doesn't really go up your nose. It's hidden behind your hand, but if you do it right – for instance, if you do a really big sniff – it's really convincing. So convincing that when Nathan saw me do it, he gasped in fright. And then he laughed. He wasn't rigid with fear any more.

He said, 'How? How did you do that?'

'Come down and I'll show you,' I said.

He swung his leg over. Held on tight and lay flat. I grabbed hold of his feet and guided him back into the loft. He was talking twenty to the dozen by now.

'How did you do that? Where's the pencil? Was that magic? Can you do magic? Are you magic?' On and on like that. Never once said thanks for saving him from certain doom.

'No. Of course I'm not magic,' I said. 'There's no such thing as magic. It's a trick.'

I was trying to get him to come downstairs so

everyone could stop worrying and climbing up ladders to look for him. But he wouldn't move until I'd proved I wasn't magic by showing him how to do the Pencil Vanish.

OK, I'll tell you how to do this now because this isn't really a trick. It's a skill. You use a skill to make a trick, just like you use words to make a joke. This skill is called 'sleight of hand'. You don't push the pencil up your nose; you let your fingers slide up the pencil and it LOOKS as if the pencil is going up your nose when it's really just going behind your fingers. As long as you're standing so that your audience can't see behind your hand.

Anyway, as we were finally coming down from the loft, Nathan spots one of those kids' magic sets sticking out of the corner of one of the unpacked boxes. On the lid was a little top hat, a pack of cards, a magic wand and the words *Hey Presto Magic Set*.

Nathan picked up the box. 'Is this it?' he said. 'Is this where you learned to do magic?'

He opened the lid slowly, slowly, like it might be the last resting place of Captain Barbossa's treasure. And there, inside, was nothing. Just the plastic tray that the bits go in, the instruction book,

one joke cigarette and a tube of fake blood. Apparently, back in the day, people's idea of fun for all the family was smoking and injuries. I was not convinced that I could amaze or amuse anyone by pretending to smoke or bleed.

I said, 'I can't really do magic. Just that one trick. Dad taught me.'

When we moved house it was the middle of summer term. So I had to leave all my old friends behind and start in a new school where I didn't know anybody. Everyone already had made friends. My first day I was refusing to go in, but Dad said, 'I probably shouldn't do this. I'm going to show you a foolproof way to make friends. Just don't mention that you got this from me. OK?' He took a pencil out of his jacket and taught me the Pencil Vanish.

That day, I walked into my new class where no one knew me. Everyone was talking in little huddles, or staring at their phones. One girl looked over at me. As soon as she did, I vanished my pencil up my nose.

The girl screamed, 'Look what she did!!! Did you see?'

She came clattering through the desks to make sure that I was all right. Ten minutes later I knew everyone in the room. The first girl who'd screamed – Lily – she's still my friend.

So the Vanishing Pencil is a cure for shyness and for getting stuck on a roof. Magic can be handy like that.

CHAPTER TEN

SCHOOL IS A TOUGH AUDIENCE

NATHAN:

The day Middy showed me the Pencil Vanish, that was like being given the answer book to life.

Middy's house is like a cousins-only Center Parcs. You get to sleep in a tent in the garden. You have picnics instead of tea. Her mum and dad are always dead busy, so you nearly can't get into trouble. At Middy's I can be all 'Wonder Time!' and 'Behold!'

Home is different. For one thing, at home you have to go to school. School is a tough audience. Or it used to be until Middy introduced me to magic. After that, everything was different.

I don't like school lunch hour. It always seems to end up with me in trouble. I tried to persuade Miss Khoshroo to let me stay indoors at dinner-time. She said fresh air and sunlight would do me good.

'I don't think so,' I said.

'Why's that then?'

I said the first thing I could think of. Sadly that was, 'I'm a vampire, Miss.'

As soon as I said it I knew it was a stupid thing to say. This used to happen to me all the time. I'd say something stupid, then realize it was stupid. I was always wishing I could realize something was stupid before I said it. It would make life loads easier.

At break the other kids followed me round making hilarious blood-sucking noises. Someone even got a crucifix down off the classroom wall and waved it at me.

I was thinking, *Right, well, I've said it now. I have to make people believe it.* So next day I filled my water bottle with tomato juice instead of water, and stood in the middle of the playground chugging it. I used the fake blood from the Hey Presto magic set to make it look like blood was dribbling down my chin. It really did look gruesome. Kids were running everywhere, screaming that I really was a vampire.

Like I said, that's kind of how magic works. You say something impossible or bonkers, and then you make it true. And people will believe you because in their hearts, they really want bonkers and impossible things to be true.

Miss Khoshroo didn't believe it though. She came steaming over the playground the minute she heard the screams, demanding to know what the noise was about. Fury made her face all creased up like a walnut. 'Oh what a surprise! The trouble is Nathan Wiley. What are you up to?'

I don't know what made me do it, but instead of answering her, I took my pencil out of my pocket and made it vanish up my nose. Every angry crease in Miss Khoshroo's face disappeared and her eyes went like saucers.

'What,' she gasped, 'did you just do!?!' She didn't wait for me to answer. She just clapped. Just one clap. Like a happy baby. 'How?' she said. 'Just how did you do that?' By now other kids were crowding around to see what was happening. They all thought she was giving me another telling-off. Instead she said, 'Do it again. Show the others.'

Now it's not easy doing a Pencil Vanish twice because 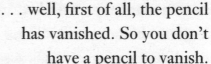 . . . well, first of all, the pencil has vanished. So you don't have a pencil to vanish. Second of all, you're stuck standing there with a pencil hidden in your hand. I bent over and did this big, horrible, rattling cough, then pretended

to cough the pencil up. The pencil shot across the playground, which made everyone scream in horror but then made them shout, *'Do it again!'*

So I did it again.

And everything changed.

I did this big, mucousy sniff for the up–my–nose bit, and this great gurgling cough for the cough–it–up bit. And all these people who'd been laughing at me and calling me an idiot, all of them suddenly thought I was a wizard.

Just because I knew how to slip a pencil behind my hand.

That's real magic.

A good magic trick makes people surprised.

A great magic trick makes them happy.

It definitely made Miss Khoshroo happy. She told me to wipe the blood off my chin and come and show the other teachers. It was the first time I'd ever been in the staff-room. The staff couldn't get enough of the Pencil Vanish. They were laughing and yelping like children. The woman from the library gave me a biscuit. From that day on, all I've ever wanted to do was surprise people into happiness.

Which is what we are doing here. I promised to bring back Blackpool Tower. And now we're going to make it happen.

CHAPTER ELEVEN

THE OLDEST TRICK IN THE BOOK

MIDDY:

At the end of every summer, the cousins all go home. The house feels really empty. End of summer is also the start of the Illuminations. Mum and Dad's busiest time. So the house feels really, really, really empty. And, just to make everything a little bit worse, Nathan sent everyone a clip of him doing his version of the Pencil Vanish. Everyone loved it. Mum was all, 'Have you SEEN this?!'

'I taught him how to do it.'

'Yeah. But not like this. This is BRILLIANT.' She showed it to Dad.

'Oh this is brilliant. Have you SEEN THIS, Middy?'

'You taught me how to do that. And I taught him.'

'Yeah, but not like this.'

Until that moment, we all knew who we were.

Brodie was the rabbit cousin.

Nathan was the complicated cousin.

And I was the magic cousin.

Now all of a sudden Nathan was the greatest thing the world had ever seen, and what was I?

When another magician's tricks are better than yours, be encouraged, not discouraged. It only means that there are more things to be learned, more wonders to perform.

Karabas the Modest, *My Secrets Revealed*

So I decided to learn a new trick. It was Dad who'd taught me the Pencil Vanish, so I started by asking him to teach me a new one. He said he didn't know any tricks.

'You taught me that one. The Pencil Vanish.'

'Oh yeah,' he said. 'But anyone can do that. It's the oldest trick in the book.'

'There's a book?' I said.

'Not literally. Although come to think of it, yeah. Probably. Probably there's a book. Try the library.'

Our library closed down years ago and I'm not allowed to go to the one in town without a grown-up. But I remembered the book inside the Hey Presto Magic Starter Set.

The fake blood had gone – I guessed Nathan had nabbed that and was probably using it to get into bother at school. But the instruction book was still there – *My Secrets Revealed* by Karabas the Modest

(Second-Best Magician of All Time).

I guess Karabas the Modest must have been the magician on the front of the book. They were so modest that their face was hidden behind a deck of cards. It was only a little book, but it had cracking tricks in it, and someone had written extra notes in the margins. They turned out to be really good too. Anyway, the first chapter was called 'The Oldest Trick in the Book – Cups and Balls'.

Cups and Balls works like this . . . The magician puts a little ball down on the table. Then puts a cup over the ball. Then lifts the cup up again and the ball has vanished! Where did it go!?! Then the magician looks under the next cup. Nothing there. Puts the cup down and lifts it up again and now there's TWO balls under that cup. Where did they come from? And it goes on like that – making balls appear and disappear. Making it look as though the balls are magically invisibly skipping from cup to cup. You keep the audience watching until they're practically dizzy from trying to keep up with the balls. You have to keep them guessing, but you have to make sure they guess wrong every time.

You might think that because it's the oldest trick in the book, Cups and Balls must be the easiest. But no. To do it properly, you've got to learn nearly all the techniques of magic – sleight of hand, French drops, good patter. I can't tell you how to do it, but I can tell you how to make it work.

Practice.

A lot of practice . . .

As Karabas says on page thirty seven of *My Secrets Revealed*:

> *Remember, if you want to amaze people, it takes time. It takes many hours of practice to make one moment of wonder.*

CAPTAIN JIMENEZ:

At this point the boy, Nathan, encouraged the girl, Middy, to demonstrate the Cups and Balls trick using three paper cups from the water fountain and some cookies instead of balls. He seemed to be under the impression that if I saw them doing a magic trick, I would believe the rest of their story.

The trick ended with the three of them each eating a cookie. At which point I realized the whole performance had been nothing but a way of hijacking my snacks.

'You know,' I said, 'I see folks doing tricks like that all the time in the old town area, doing it to gouge money out of tourists. If I'd seen you doing this downtown on Fremont Street, you would be in the

Juvenile Detention Centre right now.'

The girl said, 'Exactly.'

I said, 'What do you mean, exactly? I'm telling you that if you don't explain what you're doing here, I'm going to put you in jail.'

She said, 'That's exactly what I'm trying to do, but you keep interrupting.'

I perceived that the sugar rush from the cookies had made them tetchy and resolved to give them no more.

MIDDY:

So there I was with nothing but an empty box of tricks. What I did have though was LOADS of the most important thing – time.

In the back garden there's a space between the yellow shed and the back fence. It's full of old plant pots and stuff, which gave me the idea of doing Cups and Balls with plant pots and onions. It would be harder to do because plants pots are bigger and heavier than plastic cups. Hard is good because the harder it is to do a trick, the easier it is to believe in the magic. I tried to show Dad one day. Not being funny, I thought the way I did it was cracking. At the end he said, 'You know that onion you were looking for – it's under that plant pot.'

'Ah. But is it?' I lifted the plant pot. No onion! *Ta-dah!!!*

He said, 'Right. My mistake. If you really want an onion, there's some in the veg basket.'

'Dad, I'm trying to show you a magic trick. There was an onion, but now there isn't. Magic! See? No. You don't see. Because you're on your phone.'

Dad said, 'I just thought you wanted me to help you look for an onion. Right. Is it over now?'

To be a better magician, you have to show your trick to someone to see if it works. That person needs to be someone you can trust. A friend who will tell you the truth. I ended up face-timing Nathan. D'you know what he said? He said exactly the same thing as Dad – 'Is it over now?'

'Haven't you been watching?'

'I have,' he said. 'It was good. But I can't tell if you're finished or not. A trick needs, you know, a Wonder Time moment at the end. Otherwise you could be stuck there all day moving plant pots around.'

'I could say, *Ta-dah!* And then they'll know it's over.'

'You can't just say, *Ta-dah!* You have to earn *Ta-dah.*'

I said, 'Look, Nathan, this is really ancient, this trick. It was first performed in Ancient Egypt. You can see people doing it on murals on the walls of the tombs of the pharaohs. Being honest, the picture of that looks more like two bald men making sandcastles. But the point is that people have been doing this trick for thousands of years. In Africa, China, Japan, America and Blackpool. No one has ever complained about the ending. Until now.'

'It still needs an ending. Like when I cough up the pencil.'

'Which is horrible, by the way.'

'That's why it's an ending. People are shocked. Also, they think it went into my skull and out of my nose, which is impossible, and that's magic.'

So I thought – the audience is sitting there trying to guess how many onions there will be under the plant pot. 'What if,' I said to Nathan, 'on the last time, I give them something they could NEVER have guessed.'

'Like?' said Nathan.

'Like a banana,' I said.

'Apple is better,' said Nathan. 'A banana might be funny because bananas just are funny, but an apple is kind of the same shape as an onion. So some part of everyone's brains would be telling you a story about how an onion had turned into the apple. Which is really magic. They'll laugh when you're shuffling onions, but at the end they'll lean forward and go, 'Oh . . . but that . . . How did that . . . ? Was that magic?'

66

CHAPTER TWELVE

LET THE MAGIC BEGIN!

MIDDY:

Normally there's a lot of 'look who's grown' and 'back to back – who's tallest?' type of talk when the cousins arrive for the summer holidays. Not this year. Because no amount of human growing could even begin to compare with how much Queenie had grown. She was the size of a toddler. 'Are you sure she's a rabbit?' said Mum. 'She looks more like a small, fluffy cart horse.'

The first time I realized something was going on was when Lydia-next-door shouted over the fence, 'Is this thing on now?'

'What thing?'

'The thing on the Tobago Avenue Neighbours News app.' That was Lydia's dad, who had just popped up behind her, carrying her little brother.

'What Neighbours News app?'

'The one that tells you what's going on in the street. It said the thing was on today. Shall we just climb over?'

They were climbing over the fence when the doorbell went. Mum sent me to answer it. It was someone I'd never seen, asking me if she was too late.

'Too late for what?' I said.

'Is it through here?' She took herself through to the back garden. Before I could shut the front door, someone else arrived. Now there were more people at the front door. By the time I got into the back garden, there must have been about twenty people out there, mostly kids from up and down the avenue. They were sitting on the grass, waiting in front of the camping table where I'd set out the pots for my trick.

Lydia shouted, 'It's starting.' Everyone stared up at me expectantly.

'Go on then,' whispered Mum.

'But . . .'

In the introduction of *My Secrets Revealed*, Karabas the Modest says

> *Never underestimate the importance of boasting. If you tell people a trick is going to be astounding, they are more likely to be astounded. But remember, the most important part of the art of boasting is making sure you never, ever, ever boast about anything you can't really do. Promise me you will not call yourself 'the Great' until you're great.*

This is the opposite of Rule Five. But that's the thing about magic. You have to use your judgement.

I was planning to get the summer going by showing my cousins one little trick. Now the whole street turned out to be waiting for some kind of show. Then, right behind me, the door of the shed banged open.

And out of the shed exploded . . . what?! I didn't even know if it was human at first. All I could see was a sparkly blue cape swirling past me, with a spangly top hat on top. It threw out its arms. It boomed, '*Whoever you are . . . Whatever you are . . . Prepare. TO. BE. . . Astonished!*' A hand shot out from somewhere inside the cloak. It was holding a big shiny pencil. I said, 'Nathan?'

He didn't even look at me, just pointed at me with the pencil and said, 'A great big Tobago Avenue welcome, please, for my fabulous assistant . . . Magical Middy.'

Nathan has never had any problem with the art of boasting.

I growled, 'I'm not your assistant.'

'Whatever.'

'Tell them, I'm not your assistant.'

People were laughing. They obviously thought this argument was part of the show.

'She's not my assistant. She's my . . . well what are you then?'

'I TAUGHT you your first trick. If anyone's an assistant, it's you. And what are you wearing, by the way?'

'A cape,' he said. 'I'm a magician. Magicians wear capes.'

People were still laughing.

It was Dad who shouted, 'Let the magic begin!'

I glanced at Nathan and started to move the pots. Nathan pushed back his top hat, waved his wand and then joined in. Four hands moving the plant pots made the whole thing seem even more dizzying. Even I lost track of the hands – and two of the hands were mine.

The clapping started way before we'd finished. When we got to the bit where all the onions seemed to have disappeared, Nathan stopped, said, 'Maybe under here.' I lifted the last plant pot. This was a really big plant pot, by the way. The kind you use for little trees. There should have been an apple. But no. There instead was Queen of Tobago, happily chewing on an onion.

I nearly dropped the pot in shock. Which only made it more magic. I mean if something happens that even the magician isn't expecting, that can only be magic, can't it? And everyone could see that I wasn't expecting a rabbit.

The audience went crazy. Especially Brodie, who jumped up and yelled, 'Who said you could do magic with Queenie. Queenie is a very nervous nearly-prize-winning rescue rabbit. She . . .'

But before he could say any more, I swear Queenie got up on her haunches and took a little bow. She was loving this.

The crowd went even crazier.

'You just put her back right now!' said Brodie.

Nathan put the plant pot down over Queenie, very suddenly.

'Do not put my rabbit in a plant pot,' yelled Brodie. He barged up to the magic table and picked up the plant pot. There was nothing there.

Queenie had vanished.

This time it was Nathan who looked surprised.

'Where is she?' snapped Brodie.

'She –' gasped Nathan, trying another plant pot – 'has disappeared!'

He tried the other plant pots. Entirely rabbit-less. Every time there wasn't a rabbit, the audience applauded. I don't think any rabbit in history has got so much applause just by not being there.

No rabbit.

'Here's a clue,' I said, looking at the shed.

Brodie dived into the shed, then dived out again two seconds later, cradling the Queen of Tobago in his arms.

The audience couldn't stop cheering and clapping. Brodie was so happy and relieved he started talking like he was part of the act.

'Did you see what she did?' he said. 'She took a bow. This rabbit is a star.' He seemed to think that appearing under the plant pot had been Queenie's own idea.

Nathan had fooled me by making Queenie

appear inside a plant pot.

I had fooled him by making her reappear in her shed.

Nathan had used his unexpected cape to smuggle Queenie into the act and sneak her under the plant pot. Then Nathan spread his arms out wide and took a bow. The top hat fell off his head and he neatly caught it and twirled it around – no one could take their eyes of him. For about half a minute no one was looking anywhere else. No one was paying attention. During that time, I could have put a tutu on Queenie and done a little dance with her and no one would have noticed. Instead I snuck her back into her hutch. Which surprised Nathan.

We surprised each other.

But we astounded our audience.

We were – to be honest – astounding.

We were the Wonder Brothers.

CHAPTER THIRTEEN

RABBIT HOLES

MIDDY:

Nearly every night all through the summer – we settled down in front of YouTube and slid down a Greatest Magician of All Time rabbit hole. And no one tried to stop us because Nathan's mum said magic was the best thing that had ever happened to him. 'Before magic,' she said, 'he was so . . .'

'Bouncy,' said Mum.

'Exactly. Sometimes he'd go missing for hours on end and we'd have to go looking for him. He'd get into fights in school. But lately, he will stand in front of the mirror in the front room practising how to make a coin disappear for hours at a time. And twirling his cape. That's why I bought him the cape. And the hat. And the wand.'

Personally, I'm against all capes, and top hats and wands. They remind me of all the olden-days magicians we saw on YouTube whose act seems to be mostly shaking some poor pigeon out of your cape or just pointing at boxes. They all had glamorous assistants. I bet the glamorous assistant is always the one doing all the magic. And the so-called magician is really just a big, overdressed piece of misdirection.

'That,' said Nathan, 'is a brilliant idea. You could be the glamorous assistant.'

I said, 'And you could go and be the pigeon, you big cheese panini.'

We argued about this kind of stuff a lot.

Nathan says capes and hats and fancy jackets are really useful because they're all good places to hide things. 'There's secret pockets in the cape. And a secret pocket inside the hat. Magic is all about pockets.'

'The minute you see a top hat, you know the magician is going to do a trick. A trick should be a surprise. A top hat is like carrying a big *Warning: Trick Approaching* sign on your head. And as for a wand . . .'

Nathan really does love an argument. You could never beat him on the usefulness of wands.

'Wands?! Wands are indispensable. If you've got a wand in your left hand, people assume you haven't got anything else in your hand. It's called an acquittal. If you're hiding a coin in your left hand, but you've also got a wand in your left hand, the wand acquits the coin – see?'

We did not agree about how much stuff you need to carry if you're a magician. I like to try and fit everything in a little backpack. If Nathan had the chance, he'd prefer a set of suitcases.

All I need to do magic is a pack of cards, a few coins and some baby wipes (you need clean hands to do magic), flash papers, matches. That's it.

The things Nathan says he needs to do magic are a top hat, cane, cape, flags of all nations, invisible playing cards, glitter bombs . . . I could go on.

Things he'd LIKE to have for his act . . . doves, disappearing cabinets shaped like Egyptian sarcophaguses, a drowning cabinet, chains for escaping from.

'I love it,' he says, 'when Perplexion cuts Zenith in half. I want to have a go at that. I bet I'd be great at that.'

Magicians have been pretending to cut people in half for hundreds of years. Torrini is supposed to have cut his glamorous assistant in half in front of the Pope in Rome in 1809.

A great magic trick is a story. At the end of it, everything should be just a bit different. Cinderella's pumpkin turns into a golden carriage. The lizards turns into footmen. At the end of the story they turn back again. But

76

everyone should feel just a little bit different about pumpkins and lizards.

Karabas the Modest, *My Secrets Revealed*

I like it when you can't tell a magician is a magician until they do something magic.

That's why I like tricks like David Blaine turning a poor man's cup of coffee into a cup of money. Because the poor man has some money at the end of it. Or Criss Angel flying, because then everyone wonders if they could really fly.

'Those aren't tricks though. They're real magic.'

'There's no such thing as real magic. I can explain every one of those tricks.'

That's true by the way. Somehow whenever we watched those tricks on YouTube or whatever, I could see straight away how they worked. But whenever I tried to explain them to Nathan, he'd just put his hands in his ears and go 'La la la, not listening – you're spoiling the magic.'

'No. Seeing how a trick works is much more interesting than just watching a trick. That's where all the cleverness is. If we got to work, we could do great tricks like these. Or better ones.'

Nathan's idea for a better trick was, 'Bring two halves of a cut-in-half person on the stage at the beginning and then stick them together. THAT would be a trick.'

'But it would also be impossible.'

'Which is why it would be magic.'

Nathan understands what magic does. He just doesn't understand how it works.

Anyway, the point is all we did that summer and the next was practise magic and argue about magic.

CHAPTER FOURTEEN

WE DEMAND POCKET EQUALITY

NATHAN:

The morning of the Big Switch-On, Perplexion, Master of Mystery, made a publicity appearance at Blackpool Tower. We were there. And we saw him up close.

First we had to persuade Middy's mum to take us to work with her. 'I don't know why you're even bothered,' she said. 'Couldn't you find something more interesting than magic?'

'Serious question,' said Middy. 'What could be more interesting than magic?'

'If you're a girl, nearly anything. Plumbing, for instance.' Middy's mum is a plumber. In fact she's the boss plumber of Blackpool Tower. 'Magic is all about pockets, and girls don't have enough pockets.'

'That does not mean girls shouldn't do magic,' said Middy. 'That means girls should fight for equality of pockets.'

'Maybe,' her mum said.

Middy went off on one about great female magicians . . . for instance, Madame DeLinsky, who used to do this trick called the Bullet Catch, where a firing squad shot bullets at her and, instead of dying with her head blown off, she caught the bullets.

'The great Madame DeLinsky,' said Middy's mum, 'was not that great. If she was, she would have caught ALL the bullets. Including the bullet that someone fired at her in 1820 when she was performing for Prince Schwarzburg-Sondershausen. She missed that bullet, didn't she?'

'Yes,' said Middy.

'But it didn't miss her, did it?'

'No,' admitted Middy, 'that bullet didn't miss her.'

Middy's mum knows a surprising amount of detail about magic, but she still thinks plumbing is more interesting.

Middy's mum gave us each a piece of paper with a diagram of all the pipes in the Tower and where they lead. She said the pipes and systems in the Tower were like the veins in your body. 'Even the lifts used to be worked by water,' she said. 'Making a toilet flush when it's five hundred feet off the ground – that is real magic.'

'Mum,' said Middy, 'magic is magic, and the Master

80

of Mystery is going to be in this building any minute. We HAVE to speak to him.'

'You can go if Brodie goes with you.'

But Brodie was really happy studying the diagram. 'I like to know how to get out of a place in case something goes wrong,' he said. He took our copies for us so he would have spares in case he lost his.

We went down to the basement in a special lift that only staff are allowed to use, and Auntie Anya told us all about James Walmsley – the first plumber to work on the Tower.

'He started when the Tower was still being built,' she said. 'He was the one who made sure all the pipes were in the right place. It wasn't just toilets, by the way. There was an aquarium back then called Dr Cocker's Aquarium. It was down here, deep under the ground. Can you see the way the roof is curved? That roof was covered in shells and plaster dolphins and sea snakes so that it looked like an underwater cave. Mr Walmsley got so involved in that aquarium that he ended up living in the Tower and being put in charge of all the animals. They changed his job title from plumber to Master of Wild Beasts. He was in charge of forty polar bears. They used to have polar bears here before they realized it was cruel.'

'Can we not talk about being cruel to animals, please,' said Brodie, smoothing down Queenie's ears so she couldn't hear.

Auntie Anya explained that they used to let them out to swim in the sea when everyone had gone home. 'Think of that. Forty polar bears running up and down the beach.'

All me and Middy could think about was Perplexion, but Auntie Anya still had stuff to say about plumbing.

'At the end of any circus performance,' she said, 'they used to flood the ring with forty-two thousand gallons of water. People dressed as mermaids and mermen would do a water ballet, and then a Noah's Ark would appear and a parade of little animals – rabbits and mice – would climb on board and sail away. When that was all over, a woman called Marie Finney would dive in from a trapeze platform sixty feet up, even though the water was less than six feet deep.'

At the very, very toppermost top of the Tower there's a kind of birdcage. You have to climb this right tight winding staircase to get to it. It's like being sucked up inside a bendy straw. At the top, the wind jabs through the wires like icy swords. You can feel the Tower swaying from side to side so it's like you're flying in an iron kite. It takes a while before you get your courage up to open your eyes and look at the view. Which is sea rolling right at you from the horizon in front of you, or clouds surfing the hills behind you. Or you could look down and see the piers and fairgrounds spread out like Lego on the floor of a huge bedroom.

'During the war,' said Auntie Anya, 'they wanted to take the Tower down in case enemy planes used it as a landmark. Instead they used it as something to do with radar, and that's why there's a toilet hidden away at the very top. I'll show you.'

Middy tried to explain that we didn't want to see another toilet but her mum flushed the toilet, which drowned us out. 'Does that sound right to you?' she said. 'Is it running a bit rapid?'

I was starting to feel a bit giddy by then. I really wanted to go back down. But Auntie Anya was very flush-focused. 'It seems rapid to me,' she said. 'Let's wait till it fills up and give it another go.'

'I feel a bit giddy too,' said Brodie. 'Being honest, I might be sick.'

Auntie Anya ignored him. 'Let's take a look inside the cistern. Let's check the inflow.'

I looked at Middy and she looked at me. We could hear the sound of laughter and excitement breezing up the stairs. We were both thinking the same thing. *Perplexion. He must be here.* Just one flight of stairs way. As soon as Auntie Anya flushed that toilet, we slid away.

CHAPTER FIFTEEN

PEPPER'S GHOST

NATHAN:

If you stand on the glass floor of the Walk of Faith and look down between your feet, you can see the pavement five hundred feet below you. People dare each other to walk on it and take selfies that make it look like they're floating hundreds of feet up in the air. That afternoon it was crowded with people but no one was looking down. Everyone was watching the stairs and the lifts, waiting for Perplexion to show up. We could see the massive shoulders and tiny round sunglasses of his bodyguard. But we couldn't see Perplexion. There was a woman in a long black coat in the middle of the crowd. Without saying anything, she dropped her coat and threw her hands in the air. As soon as she took the coat off, I recognized her – it was Zenith.

Under the coat, she was wearing a dress so covered in sequins that, in the afternoon sun, it looked like it was on fire.

'Hello, Blackpool!' she said. 'I am Zenith and I'm here to ask you to welcome the Master of Mystery himself. It's . . . Perplexion!!!!!'

Everyone looked at the stairs, expecting him to come that way. But then they realized she was pointing downwards. Because there was Perplexion, under our feet, looking up at us from UNDER the glass floor. FLOATING four hundred feet in the air.

'Mirrors,' whispered Middy in my ear. 'He's doing it with mirrors. A very old illusion. It's called Pepper's Ghost. After John Pepper who invented it in the 1860s for a production of a play by Charles Dickens, who—'

'Middy, stop spoiling the magic.'

When I looked back, Perplexion had slipped from view under the bit of the floor where Zenith's coat was lying. She picked up the coat and somehow there was Perplexion, standing right in front of us.

As soon as he was definitely, really there, standing on the glass, everyone rushed forward. They wanted to touch him to see if he was really real.

The bodyguard did a good job of pushing everyone back with his shovel-sized hands.

A group of girls all dressed in black started chanting, 'One. More. Trick. One. More. Trick.'

Perplexion smiled at them, with pity in his eyes. Being fair, the guy had just somehow floated up from the ground and through a glass floor. What more did they want?

Zenith raised her arms again. Got to say, that was a good attention grabber. Every time she did it, her dress flashed fire.

'Perplexion does not do tricks,' she said. 'He performs wonders.'

Perplexion's signature trick is sawing Zenith in half. It's not like he can ask the audience if they have a spare chainsaw.

'One. More. Trick. One. More. Trick.'

'The lady,' said the bodyguard, 'said no.' His voice was deep. Like chip shop gravy rolling through the room.

86

All the crowd wanted was a bit of magic. And I had my bag full of magic . . . top hat, flags of all nations all of it. So it just sort of seemed to me this was it. Our once-in-a-lifetime chance. I didn't have to think it over. There wasn't actually time to explain this to Middy. '*Whoever you are*,' I said. '*Whatever you are . . .*' You know the rest. 'My assistant and I are here to bring you a little bit of magic.'

You could tell Middy wasn't happy about being called my assistant by the way she bawled, 'I am NOT his assistant!' For some reason, everyone thought this was funny. They laughed, and the laugh was that electrical-current moment. We had an audience.

We were doing a show.

Perplexion smiled down at us. The kind of smile a snake gives a mouse before swallowing it. Zenith did not smile. She bent down and hissed so quietly no one else could hear her, 'Go back to your mummy. No one dares do magic when Perplexion is in the room.'

I pointed out that my mum wasn't in the room. Or even in Blackpool. Then I took out a pencil, looked at Middy, and – without saying a word to each other – we both stuffed the pencils up our noses. People stood back in horror at the sound of snot swirling round inside our heads as the pens shot up into our brains. Some of them screamed when we shot the pencils back out again.

I thought Perplexion might be cross enough finally to speak. But instead, he just pointed to us and then clapped. Seeing him do it, Zenith did the same. Everyone else clapped too. Somehow that made it look like the whole thing had been Perplexion's idea and they were sort of applauding him, not us.

'Ladies and gentlemen –' Zenith smiled as though this was all her idea – 'that may be the oldest trick in the book, but I think they did it really well. Don't you agree?'

'In fact,' said Middy, 'the oldest trick in the world was by Dedi of Djed-Sneferu (it's in Egypt). The story goes he did it for a pharaoh in Egypt thousands of years ago, and it was a shocker. Listen to this, he took a duck and a chicken, cut their heads off and swapped them round. So the duck had a chicken's head, and the chicken had a duck's head.' I thought Middy was just saying this because it was interesting, but it turned out that this was a smart little piece of misdirection. 'And after he'd swapped the heads round, he swapped them back. No one knows how he did it. Unless –' she looked at Perplexion – 'you do?'

Perplexion just smiled. Mysteriously.

Everyone was clapping and getting their phones out to film us. Even Perplexion clapped us. But when he did, his hands burst into flames and blue smoke curled up from his sleeves and basically went straight into my lungs. Everyone whooped and the clapping got louder.

I tried to cough the smoke out of my lungs. I shouted, 'What are you clapping him for!?! He nearly burned my top. Plus that's not magic. That's easy. All you have to do is—'

'Now, now.' Zenith smiled, pushing me aside. 'Magicians never tell. It's the rules.'

'Magicians,' I said, 'don't set fire to other magicians. That's in the rules too.'

Everyone was still laughing and clapping. Basically we were going down a storm.

So that's how the Wonder Brothers came to perform to great acclaim at the Home of Magic, Blackpool Tower.

Also, I stole Perplexion's watch.

CHAPTER SIXTEEN

THE MAGIC CODE

CAPTAIN JIMENEZ:

For the record: One of the children has admitted stealing, using so-called magic to deprive people of their property. Namely, a watch.

The boy Nathan said, 'I didn't steal it. I vanished it. It's not hard to remove a watch. You just have to practise. I practised. A lot. Do you want me to do it to you, Captain?'

I said that, no, I did not want him to steal my watch. But when I said that, I saw that he was holding my watch up and smiling at me. I found this more than somewhat testing and did warn them that the more they talked, the more trouble they seemed to be talking themselves into.

MIDDY:

There are rules in magic.

In the back of *My Secrets Revealed*, someone with neat handwriting has written down all the rules of magic.

1. NEVER tell anyone how you do your tricks.
2. NEVER do a trick in public until you've learned to do it perfectly. If you do a trick badly, people will be able to see how you did it and you will therefore be in breach of Rule One.
3. NEVER perform a trick without telling your audience it is a trick. Magic is not the same as lying. The point of lying is to deceive. The point of magic is wonder. Magic is honest deceit.
4. NEVER refer to yourself as 'the Great' or 'the Astounding' or 'the Mysterious' unless you are great, astounding and mysterious. That's lying, and therefore a breach of Rule Three.
5. NEVER be flashy. Magic is not about showing people how clever you are. People do not trust boastful or flashy people. Wonder comes from trust.
6. NEVER let your eyes look where you don't want the audience to look. The audience is always paying attention. Your job is to make sure that they are paying attention to the wrong thing. This is called misdirection and it's the most important part of magic.

7. NEVER forget, if one magician fools another, that is the highest form of magic. And the fooled magician must show respect to the fooler.

8. NEVER, EVER, EVER promise that you can do a piece of magic if you are not completely sure, sure you can do it. NOT EVER. JUST DON'T. THAT IS THE WORST.

When Nathan stole Perplexion's watch, that was definitely a breach of Rule Three.

'He stole our applause, so I removed his watch from his wrist. He didn't feel a thing. That's a magic trick.'

'It's only a magic trick if you give it back, you massive flapjack,' I said. 'If you walk off with it, it's a robbery. Give me the watch. I'm going to give it back.'

He put his hand in his pocket and pulled out a whole fistful of watches.

'Nathan!' I said. 'What did you think you were doing?'

'I removed other people's watches too.'

'Why!?!' I said.

Nathan said, 'He's a magician. I thought he'd be hard to fool. So I practised first. On the audience.'

I thought he'd committed a crime. He was really more like a crimewave. 'Give them to me.'

I strolled off with the stolen watches.

'I'm going back in there,' I said, 'to turn your crime into a magic trick.'

Back on the glass floor, the monster bodyguard in the suit was trying to muscle Perplexion towards the lift. I shouted after him, 'Time does fly when you're enjoying yourself, Mr Perplexion . . .' It sounds like a weird thing to say, but weird is an attention-getter.

He looked back at me.

'But where does it fly TO?'

I could have just held up his watch and given it back, but that wouldn't be doing magic. That would just be admitting to a crime. Instead, I got myself right up alongside him, reached up into his sticky-up hair, and said, 'I think you've let it go to your head. Ha ha!' And then I palmed the watch so it looked like I was pulling it out of his hair.

For a second he forgot to be Perplexion, Master of Mystery, and he turned into just another annoyed watch-owner. He grabbed the watch out of my hand and nearly, nearly, nearly spoke, but caught

himself just in time. He just glared.

'But. Wait!' Nathan bounced up next to me. 'There's more!' He called. 'Look!' He pointed at Perplexion's hair. Everyone looked. While they were all looking at the spiky blond crest, Nathan palmed a watch into my hand.

Perplexion seemed too surprised to move.

I said, 'I can see it. If you let me . . .' I reached up, with the watch that Nathan had slipped me still concealed in my hand, and pretended to find it hidden in Perplexion's hair. I held it up and asked if anyone recognized it. It belonged to a girl in black.

'You stole my watch!' she squealed. 'Perplexion stole my watch!' She made it sound like it was the honour of a lifetime to have your watch stolen by Perplexion. While she was the centre of attention, Nathan palmed me another watch, while I shouted, 'And yours was not the only one . . .'

Perplexion stepped away. He definitely didn't like people messing with his hair. But I pulled another watch from it. Zenith snarled at me to leave his hair alone.

'But surely Mr Perplexion,' I said, pulling another watch out of his coiffeur, 'doesn't want to leave with this?' And then another watch. 'Or this?' And another.

By now a queue of people was forming to get their watches back. I'd pull them out of his hairdo, and Nathan would give them back to their owners. He handed them over like certificates on school prize-giving night.

When the last watch had been handed back, d'you know what Perplexion did? He stepped back and took a bow. A proper hands-in-the-air, head-nearly-touching-the-ground bow. And everyone applauded him. Him. Not us. We did the trick, and he got the applause. He really did steal our applause.

Then the bodyguard started to push Perplexion through the crowd. Not towards the lift but towards the stairs that led up to the birdcage. Mum was standing there on the bottom step as if she was waiting for him. They went off upstairs together.

We wiggled through the crowd. The bodyguard tried to stop us following him up the stairs, but Brodie showed him the Access All Areas badge Mum had given him. The one that authorized her to see all plumbing.

Up in the birdcage, Mum was waiting outside the special World War Two toilet.

'Perplexion needed a wee,' she said. 'This was the nearest.'

We heard the toilet flush. Mum's face flushed too with pride. Then the toilet door opened. And there was no one in there.

Perplexion had vanished.

'He does like to vanish,' she said.

CHAPTER SEVENTEEN

DON'T GO FAR . . .

BRODIE:

None of this has got anything to do with the Tower.

The most important point is, on the Big Switch-On night, the Tower vanished. And the next morning Nathan and Middy were on the TV, promising to bring it back again. A couple of hours later the clip of them saying that was everywhere. I mean *everywhere*.

When we got home we turned the TV on and there was the reporter from Lancashire Hot Press saying,

'We asked Perplexion for a comment on the disappearance – was it a magic trick? – but Perplexion doesn't like to talk to mortals. However we DID manage to get an interview with the Master of Mystery's glamorous assistant, Zenith.'

When Zenith popped up on the screen and said Perplexion had no comment to make, the reporter said, *'What about the children who said they could bring back the Tower. Any comment about them?'*

Zenith purred, *'If they do that, that really would be magic.'*

MIDDY:

When I saw that report, I got raging. Nathan didn't even seem a tiny bit bothered. 'Look!' he said, 'We're on telly! Does anyone fancy some cheese on toast?'

I said, 'Nathan, what's the most important rule in the Magic Code? The most important rule in the magic code is:

8. NEVER, EVER, EVER promise that you can do a piece of magic if you are not completely sure you can do it. NOT EVER. JUST DON'T. THAT IS THE WORST.

'And you broke it. You broke it, and Perplexion – the greatest magician on earth – knows you broke it.'

Nathan said, 'But we are going to bring the Tower back. It was in my dream.'

It was the first I'd heard about his dream. The one where we were going to perform on the biggest stage in Las Vegas. Nathan said the dream was so real it felt like it had really happened.

'We're two kids in Blackpool, Lancashire. How could we possibly pop up on a big stage in Las Vegas, America?'

'Magic,' he said.

'There's no such thing as magic.'

'You're always saying that.'

'Because it's true.'

'But every time you see a new trick, before you work it out, there's a minute, isn't there, when you think – was that magic?'

I didn't say anything because he was sort of right. There really is always a moment when you see a new trick and you think *oh! But how!?* And you kind of want it to be real magic. But that was beside the point.

Nathan stood up with his palms out wide the way magicians do when they're about to start a show, to prove that they're not hiding anything in their hands. 'If a magician fools another magician,' he said, 'the magician who was fooled has to show respect to the magician who fooled them. That's in the rules too.'

It actually is. It's Rule Seven.

'We fooled Perplexion,' said Nathan, 'so he has to talk to us.'

I pointed out that Perplexion very famously doesn't talk to anyone.

'Well he has to see us then. We are going to see Perplexion and we are going to ask him politely to put the Tower back. What do you say? Got to be worth a go?'

I had to admit that it really did have to be worth a go.

'Where are you two going?' asked Dad when he saw us leaving with our magic bags.

I said we were just going out for a bit.

'Going to bring the Tower back? Make sure you don't leave it where I could trip over it.' Dad and his jokes. 'Brodie, go with them. Keep an eye on them.'

'OK,' sighed Brodie.

'Don't let them go far,' said Dad. 'Tea's nearly ready. Hear me?'

I said, 'Yes, Dad.'

'What did I just say?'

'Don't go far,'

'Why?'

'Because we've got to be back for tea.'

And then we went to Las Vegas.

CHAPTER EIGHTEEN

PERPLEXION IS HERE

NATHAN:

We didn't know where exactly in Blackpool Perplexion was staying. But round the back of the Grand Imperial Hotel there was a lorry parked. It had a big painting of Perplexion holding up a chainsaw on the side. We thought that was a pretty good clue.

His monster bodyguard was standing there, chatting to someone from the hotel and eating two Greggs steak bakes. One in each hand. He had a T-shirt on under his jacket that had *Perplexion Is Here* written across it in blue spangles.

'See?' I said. 'He's here. It says so.'

The back door of the truck was open and we could see inside. There was the painted Egyptian sarcophagus that made people disappear. There was the giant chainsaw he used to cut people in half. There was a rack of spangly outfits and silvery trousers. When she saw all this stuff, Middy was purely distracted with happiness. It seemed to pull her nearer and nearer to the back of the truck like a spell.

But even Middy wasn't as interested as Queenie. She wriggled out of Brodie's arms and bounced off into the truck. Brodie followed her, and we followed Brodie.

Middy was hypnotized. She was drifting all around the place, *oohing* and *ahhhing* like a kid in Santa's grotto. 'What will happen to it all –' she sighed – 'now that he's going to stop doing magic?'

Storage was something Perplexion might not need to worry about, the rate his equipment was being gnawed into sawdust by Queenie. She was nibbling away at the corner of the big Egyptian sarcophagus. Brodie wasn't even trying to stop her.

'I've always wanted to see a sarcophagus for real,' he said, leaning right inside. 'In *Tomb Warriors*, you get an extra life if you can get in and out of one before . . .'

His voice faded away as the lid closed. When it clicked shut, the pharaoh winked at us. That did not make me feel tranquil. Brodie knocked on the lid from inside, shouting, 'Let us out. Queenie is scared.'

So we opened the lid again and . . . the box was empty. Brodie and Queenie had vanished.

Wonders!

What we were looking at was a vanishing box, as invented by John Nevil Maskelyne back in the 1800s. Well not invented. Back in history, fraudsters and swindlers used this kind of thing to make people believe in ghosts and spirits. Maskelyne said that was wrong because magic is honest deception, not *deception* deception. So he started using the vanishing box in his magic act. Middy explained that he offered a £500 reward to anyone who could figure out how it worked.

'Shall I tell you how it worked?' said Middy.

Brodie – reappearing just behind us – said, 'Will he give us five hundred pounds if you do?'

It was the sudden reappearance of Brodie that made us all turn round. That's when we saw the bodyguard had finished his steak bakes and was standing in the doorway, shining a torch into the truck.

Middy said, 'Don't worry. We're just three kids looking for Perplexion. We really need to talk to him.'

'Three kids. And a rabbit,' said Brodie.

The big man nodded his head as if he was agreeing with us. But then he carried on nodding his head. He wasn't nodding at us. He was nodding along to music on his headphones. He couldn't hear us. He didn't even know we were there.

The doors of the truck banged shut. A lock scraped into place, and when the door opened, we were in Las Vegas.

So you see, we really did get here by magic.

CHAPTER NINETEEN

THE EXTRAORDINARY
EXPLODING BOX

MIDDY:

You see, this is what happened.

When Mr Steak Bake closed the door, everything went dark. Then the truck began to shake.

'We're moving,' said Brodie. 'Where are we going? Where's Queenie? We have to make this stop.' He started banging on the back door of the truck, shouting to be let out.

I pointed out that since the truck was moving, there definitely wouldn't be anyone outside the door. We should knock at the other end – then the driver might hear us. We scrambled through all Perplexion's magic equipment. Nathan kept telling us to calm down. He said the driver was probably only driving up to Bonny Street to get more steak bakes.

We did a lot of yelling and banging on the truck

wall at the driver's end. We listened for a reply, but nothing. We had to admit that if the driver was really looking for steak bakes, he had definitely taken a wrong turn.

Brodie made it really clear that he didn't like being locked in the truck. He pointed out a lot of the bad things about being locked in a moving truck.

'What if we run out of oxygen? What if we crash? There must be a way out? There must be a phone signal.' He spent a lot of time clambering around looking for a phone signal and searching for a way out. 'I promised,' he said, 'that I'd get you back for tea.'

While Brodie was busy not panicking, Nathan was poking around. A great big arch of light bulbs suddenly flared into life. We all jumped except Nathan, who took a little bow and said, 'That should throw a little light on things.'

In the brightness of the lights, you could see that the place was just stacked with Perplexion's stage props. I was thrilled to be so close to them, I didn't actually mind that we were locked in the back of a truck on our way to some unknown destination. I was happy studying away at how all his tricks and gimmicks work. If I was never going to see Perplexion's act, then being allowed to get a close look at all his stage stuff was the next best thing.

There was a glass tank that looked like it was full of water but wasn't. It just had a kind of double-glazing with water in between the panes of glass. It was a trick tank that made it look as

though you were under water when really you were just sitting behind a kind of vertical puddle. I shouldn't have told you that. It's giving someone's trick away. Please forget I said that.

I found what looked like a small suitcase and undid the catch. Then the air exploded with a sound like R2-D2 dropped from a great height. I fell flat on my back and the others yelled in fright. The small suitcase had expanded into a metal box the size of a washing machine. It took a minute for me to get my breath back. But when I did, I lost my breath all over again.

Because I knew what I was looking at. 'Do you know what this is?' I said.

'Is it the big metal box of death?' said Nathan.

'This is De Kolta's Exploding Box!' I squealed.

'De Kolta can keep it,' said Brodie, 'whoever he is. It nearly killed you.'

De Kolta was a French magician hundreds of years ago. He invented the Vanishing Lady and the Vanishing Birdcage and this – the Exploding Box.

Brodie sighed. 'Can we make sure it doesn't explode again?'

'This was one of the most famous tricks in history,' I said. 'He used to bring this little box onto the stage, then do a bit of hocus pocus, the box would expand – like it did just then – and his wife would step out of it.'

If you're wondering how his wife fitted inside the little box, I can't tell you. But the trick was really, really dangerous because the box was metal and the springs that opened it moved really fast. It could knock you senseless. Even Houdini couldn't find a way of doing it safely. It's one of the most dangerous tricks ever in this world.

The truck suddenly dropped and everything shuddered and rang. It was like being inside a huge bell.

'I think we've stopped,' said Brodie.

'I think we've fallen down a mineshaft,' said Nathan.

Brodie dashed to the door, saying that someone was bound to let us out now. 'Hello! Hello! We're in here!' How can there still be no phone signal?'

Nathan suggested starting up the chainsaw and cutting our way out of the truck. It would be nice if he didn't get so excited by the possibility of disaster. I pushed past him and crouched down to see if I could see anything through the gap at the bottom of the door.

'What's there?' said Brodie. 'Can you see anyone?'

He started banging and shouting again. No one answered. Because there was no one out there. There was nothing out there but darkness.

Then the truck began to shake. Not shaking like when it was driving, but shaking all over, as though someone had driven us into a giant dishwasher and turned it on. And the noise – the noise was like being inside a giant vacuum cleaner.

A few seconds later and our ears were popping like on a rollercoaster. Then everything went quiet. The walls carried on vibrating, but not as much as before. There was a background hum. I'd had this feeling before somewhere.

It was Brodie who said, 'Are we . . . ? Do you think we are . . . ? I'm not sure, but . . . I think we're flying. In a plane.'

'I can't believe,' said Nathan, 'that the very first time in my whole life I go on an airplane, I don't get to see out of the window.'

Brodie carried on looking for some kind of emergency exit even when I pointed out that it would be no use without a parachute. We'd just have to wait until we landed.

'Landed where though?' said Brodie. 'Where are we going?'

'I DON'T KNOW! Well it's all Perplexion's stuff, so we're probably going to wherever Perplexion is.'

'But, but,' said Brodie, 'I said we'd be home for tea.'

As soon as he said that, we noticed we were hungry. We also noticed that there was no food. Except the sticks of rock I had in my magic bag for my Rock and Roll trick. I said I didn't think it was a good idea to eat our own act. But what option did we have?

Nathan did find one of those tiny fridges. 'Look!' he yelled. 'It's a feast.' This is Nathan's idea of a feast: two cans of Diet Coke, one not-very-recent cheese panini and a box of custard doughnuts.

So that was the in-flight catering. For in-flight entertainment, I thought the best thing was to keep busy. I decided to have a go at improving the Exploding Box. I won't go into detail. I'll just say, if you make the box out of something less life-threatening than metal, it works a treat.

I found a stack of boxes in the corner of the truck, full of little things that magicians need – coins, thumb tips, sequins, gimmicks – I just had to try building it.

I sorted all the coins and sequins into some plastic bags I found and I made my own De Kolta's box. When I finished, I had something that looked like a school lunchbox but blew up to the size of a big suitcase.

Ta–dah!

By this time the others were feeling too cold to appreciate it. Even Queenie was shivering under her thick coat of fur.

The only warmth we could find was Perplexion's spangly jackets and silvery trousers. Nathan nabbed a cape, obviously. I mean, he really does love a cape. He kept himself warm by swirling it round.

I got a bit excited about just how many secret pockets there were in the jackets. Tiny pockets inside the cuffs for hiding rings and coins in. A pocket inside the front that you could probably hide the small fridge in. In fact, mine had a piece of twine with flags of all nations pinned to it. I bunched the rest up into a pillow so I could have a lie-down. The other jackets also had flags in, so we made a pile of Perplexion costumes. Nathan turned out the lights and the three of us snuggled around Queenie and went to sleep.

We only woke up when the sarcophagus slid past us like a boat and gonged into the door.

We'd landed.

*

We're all different, aren't we? If you accidentally lock three people in a truck for a few hours, they will all have different ideas about what to do when a stranger comes to let them out.

'We should hide,' said Nathan, climbing into the sarcophagus.

Brodie said, 'No! We should explain to whoever opens the door that there's been a bit of a mix-up and could they please, please phone Uncle Kevin.'

But all I felt was a tingle of hope that maybe Perplexion himself would come through that door.

In the end it didn't matter what any of us thought. It was Queenie who decided our fate.

CHAPTER TWENTY

WE DEFINITELY WILL NOT BE HOME FOR TEA

MIDDY:

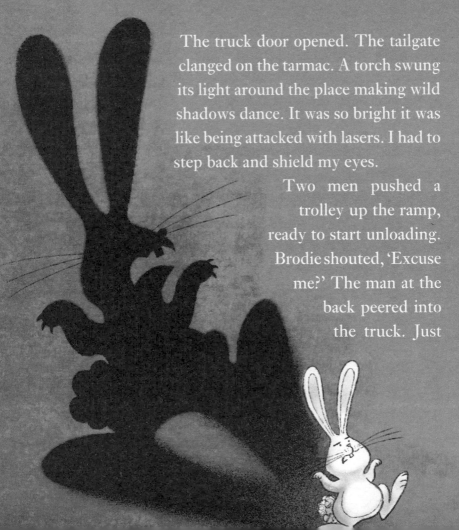

The truck door opened. The tailgate clanged on the tarmac. A torch swung its light around the place making wild shadows dance. It was so bright it was like being attacked with lasers. I had to step back and shield my eyes.

Two men pushed a trolley up the ramp, ready to start unloading. Brodie shouted, 'Excuse me?' The man at the back peered into the truck. Just like our eyes weren't used to the light, theirs weren't used to the dark. He shone his torch into the truck.

There was Queenie sitting in front of the sarcophagus. When the torchlight hit her, she must have thought she was back in the spotlight. She sat up on her haunches with her ears high in the air and made a little bow. Queenie is a large rabbit. But her shadow, in the torchlight, was not large. It was gigantic. Even I got a fright.

The man with the torch dropped it with a yelp. When he did that, the torch shone up onto the face of the sarcophagus. It was a shame that Nathan was hiding in there, because when he peeped through the eyeholes, they moved. A lot. Which frightened the men even more.

Then Brodie called out, 'Hello? Who's there?'

And before we had a chance to say or do anything else, the men ran off, leaving the truck doors wide open.

NATHAN:

When we looked out we were in some kind of warehouse. We shouted, 'Hello?' a few times, but no one came. So we left. We walked out into an alley, where the brightest sunlight we'd ever seen was ricocheting off the walls. We kept having to stop and blink. Then, at the end of the alley, we saw it . . . Blackpool Tower.

But not in Blackpool.

So someone *had* moved Blackpool Tower.

Wonders!

MIDDY:

Except it wasn't the Blackpool Tower. I could see that straight away. It was the Eiffel Tower. The Eiffel Tower is tall and skinny and elegant, standing on tiptoe like a high-heeled shoe. Our Tower is wider and shorter and cheery and chubby, and it's standing on top of a circus. So obviously we were in Paris.

In fact, there was even a sign saying, *Welcome to the Paris*.

Only Brodie wasn't sure about it. 'I'm not sure,' he said. 'Why would the *Welcome to Paris* sign be in English and not, say, French? And why does it say *the Paris* instead of just *Paris*?'

'Because this is THE Paris,' said Nathan. 'There are other cities called Paris, but this one is THE Paris, the original and best. Look. Look! See that big stone arch? That's the Arc de Triomphe!'

'That,' said Brodie, 'is a LOT smaller than I thought it would be.'

'I'll tell you something,' said Nathan. 'It smells like Blackpool.'

Fair enough, the air did smell of frying doughnuts and fizzy drinks, just like the promenade at home. But back home a salty sea breeze would be blowing those smells around your head. Not here. The air was still and hot. When we stepped out of the shade, it hit us like a hammer. Everyone was wearing shorts and flat shoes. Everyone was walking really quickly. I had the feeling there was a big party going on somewhere, but no one knew exactly where.

Nathan said, 'Why is it so hot?'

It really was hot. I took off my spangly jacket. Brodie took off his sparkly tailcoat. Nathan couldn't take off his cape because he loved it too much.

We found a fountain, which was exactly the best thing to find. We sat beside it for ages, splashing our faces and dangling our feet in it. We strolled along the cobbled street trying to stay in the shade of the palm trees.

'THE Paris is disappointing,' said Nathan. 'One Eiffel Tower, one fountain, one cobbled street and a load of old traffic.'

'Do you get the feeling,' asked Brodie, 'that we've walked a really, really long way? Because it looks to me like around the next corner is Egypt.'

A few hundred yards up the road, looking towards us over the roofs of the passing cars, was definitely the Sphinx. Its huge stone face shimmered in the heat of the traffic. When the lights changed and the cars stopped, we could see its massive lion shoulders rising up in front of a huge pyramid. There was a big flashing sign in front of it saying *Luxor*.

'I'm very sure,' said Brodie, 'that Luxor is a place in Egypt, which would explain all the palm trees.' There were palm trees along the pavement on both sides of the road. I hadn't really noticed them until then.

Brodie looked at his phone to check. But it was

dead. All our phones were dead.

All this time we had been walking in the same direction as the crowd, but now the crowd had stopped walking and turned into a queue. A traffic jam of people. We sent Brodie up to the front to see what we were accidentally queueing for. It turned out to be a sign.

'They're queueing up to take selfies under it,' said Brodie.

And what did that sign say? It said *Welcome to Las Vegas, Nevada, USA.*

'We are definitely,' said Brodie, 'not going to be home for tea.'

CHAPTER TWENTY-ONE

AN HONEST LIE

NATHAN:

I said, 'We're in Las Vegas. That explains everything!'

Brodie said he wasn't sure. 'I don't think it explains,' he said, 'what we're doing here.'

'Or how we're going to get home,' said Middy.

'Or what we're going to eat,' said Brodie.

'Or drink,' said Middy.

Brodie wanted to find a police station and explain that we'd come to America by accident and could they help us get home.

But I said, 'Was it an accident though? In my dream, we were in Las Vegas. We were on-stage. We were stars. Now here we are. In Las Vegas. Without even trying. *As if by magic.* Surely that must mean something. Surely we should wait and see what happens. If it all gets a bit sticky, we can go to the police then.'

'Not sure,' said Brodie. 'Not sure I want to wait till things get sticky.'

'What are you even worried about?'

'Just the usual things. Food, money, shelter.'

'We're magicians,' I said. 'If you can do magic, people nearly always throw money at you. And food sometimes. Though that's not always in a good way.'

'Do magic where?' said Middy.

'Middy,' I said. 'Give your head a shake. Where are you standing right now?'

'In a queue,' she said.

'Don't think of it as a queue. Think of it as an audience. We're the Wonder Brothers. We're always ready for magic. And Las Vegas is ready for us to amaze it.'

MIDDY:

Real magic is an honest lie. You lie – for instance, about where a playing card is hidden – in order to tell the greater truth: that life is more wonderful than you know. That's the honest lie. A real trick doesn't trick people. It fools them, but it doesn't make a fool of them. It makes them happier and wise. Anyone who uses magic to make a fool of someone is not a magician, but a con artist.'

Karabas the Modest, *My Secrets Revealed*

Nathan's idea of doing a magic show for the people in the queue was a good one. It's just a pity that someone else thought of it first. A woman in a Stars and Stripes top hat was just a few yards up the line, doing Cups and Balls on a little table.

There are loads of different versions of Cups and Balls. There's mine, obviously, with the plant pots. In Japan they do it in time to music so it looks like a little magical dance. There's a little girl in China who does it so fast the the cups and balls look like they're blurring into each other. You can look her up on YouTube. In India, performers sometimes sit on the floor, with the audience looking down, which is really hard because they can see everything. In magic, the angle is everything.

The woman in the Stars and Stripes top hat was doing it with sea shells and little painted peas. The big difference between her and the little girl in China or the musical version is that she was doing it to steal money off people. She wasn't a magician. She was a con artist.

Con artists have been using magic to steal money from unsuspecting fools since Ancient Greek times. It works like this. The con artist shuffles a painted pea between three cups. Then bets anyone in the audience that they can't tell where the pea is. Always someone bets, but just in case they don't, the con artist has a mate in the audience – they're called a stooge –

who gets the betting going.

Anyway, at first the con artist lets the unsuspecting fools win a few times so that they get even less suspecting and start to bet proper money. When a fool places a really big bet, the con artist disappears the pea and collects all the money. Like I said, it's been around for thousands of years, but people still fall for it, and even though it's been around for thousands of years, Nathan had never heard of it.

That's how the trouble started.

Because he didn't know it was a con. Nathan didn't realize that the woman in the top hat was letting the audience win on purpose. He just thought she wasn't very good at Cups and Balls.

And he decided to help her.

So, when someone in the audience won a bet, he shouted, 'Miss, you're doing it all wrong.'

The woman tipped her top hat at Nathan, smiled and said, 'I'll try again. Maybe I'll get it right this time. Anyone care to chance a few dollars?'

A man with a very long body and a very long beard came forward, put ten dollars on the table and watched right close while Stars and Stripes shuffled the shells.

'You're letting him see!' shouted Nathan. 'Anyone can tell the pea is under the—'

'Shush,' said Stars and Stripes. 'Give me a break here.'

But the guy with the long beard guessed right and won twenty dollars. When he came forward to collect the money, a bunch of his mates came with him. They were all like him – heads halfway to the sky, beards nearly touching the floor. They looked like a school trip for wizards.

'You wouldn't consider,' said Stars and Stripes, 'giving a gal one more chance to win the money back?

Double or quits?'

The man with the long beard chewed his hairy lip thoughtfully. So did his mates. The guy put all his winnings back on the table and slapped another twenty dollars on top of that.

Stars and Stripes looked up at the beardy men. 'So there's a hundred and fifty dollars. Any of you guys care to join him?'

They never said a word, just looked at the first guy and nodded their beards, and all added a few dollars to the pile. So now there was a lot of money on that table.

'This,' said Stars and Stripes, 'is starting to look kind of serious. It's time for me to concentrate.' She took off her hat. She shook out her hair, put her hat down on the table and started to shuffle the shells.

'That's more like it!' Nathan smiled. Every beardy head swung around to look at him. Nathan shouted at them. 'Don't look at me! Watch the shells!'

They looked back at the shells. Stars and Stripes had already stopped shuffling. It was time for the beardy guys to choose a shell. They still didn't talk, but they scrunched up their hairy caterpillar eyebrows. Maybe they were airdropping their thoughts to each other.

Finally the first one pointed to the shell on the left.

Stars and Stripes said, 'Is he correct, people? Have I finally beaten this hawk-eyed gentleman? Sir, would you like to lift the shell yourself? Unless . . . Wait . . .

Are you sure you won't change your mind?'

Anyone who knew anything about the Cups and Balls could have told the beardy guys that it would make no difference which shell they chose because the pea wasn't under any of the shells any more. Stars and Stripes had flicked the painted pea under her top hat. The beardy blokes didn't know that. They looked from shell to shell, beards twitching like the tails of hungry panthers trying to decide what to eat. Finally they decided on the one on the left.

'No!' yelled Nathan, 'You're going to lose all your money!'

Too late. Stars and Stripes had already flipped the left-hand shell over and swiped the money into her pocket all in one movement. There was no pea under the shell.

'It's under the hat,' said Nathan.

All those caterpillar eyebrows, all those panther beards turned towards him. When the first guy spoke, his voice was so deep you could hear it through your feet.

'What,' he growled through his big cat beard, 'is really going on here?'

'I was only trying to help,' said Nathan.

'You kept saying she was no good at this. You encouraged me to bet.' All the other beards nodded.

'Then at the crucial moment,' said Nathan, 'you

distracted me! I looked away from the shells.'

'The minute I bet big . . . I lose,' growled the beard. 'This woman is not a street magician. She's a phoney. A cheat. And you, sir, are her stooge.'

'Stooge,' agreed the others, crowding round Nathan, trapping him in a net of angry beards.

A really, truly good magic trick brings everyone together in a moment of wonder. Nathan had brought everyone together in a moment of muddle and rage. I've never seen anyone make so many enemies so quickly.

Somehow it was my job to save him.

I slipped behind the table with the shells and peas on it and I called, '*Whoever you are . . . Whatever you are* . . . Our young friend here . . . says that the pea is under the hat. Let's see if he's telling the truth. Let's look under the hat.'

Stars and Stripes looked like she might explode with fear or fury. But before I picked up the hat, I just casually slapped my lunchbox trick down on the table.

This is what the crowd saw next.

The second the lunchbox hit the table – *bang* – it went off. It erupted from a lunchbox big enough for a sandwich into something big enough for a school picnic in an instant. It happened so fast, people blinked, jumped back, gasped. One second later, the lid of the big box flipped back and there was a massive rabbit wearing the controversial Stars and Stripes top hat.

To the people in the queue, it looked like the big rabbit had been hidden away inside the little lunchbox. That would be amazing with any rabbit, but with a rabbit the size of Queenie, it was astounding. When her head popped out in the top hat, everyone smiled. No one was expecting it. They'd been expecting a pea.

So no one was interested in beating up Nathan any more.

So, you know, *Ta-dah*.

CHAPTER TWENTY-TWO

LUCKY SILVER DOLLAR

MIDDY:

This is how I did it: I'd taken De Kolta's Exploding Box and turned it into something less lethal – Middy's Exploding Lunch Box. The box blows up so fast that everyone naturally looks away or shuts their eyes and their brains are just full of 'Whaaaat is happening?!' It's easy to stick something inside the box. So I stuck Queenie in, and right on cue, Queenie popped out again, as though she'd always been in there. She is a right good performer.

A massive rabbit in a hat was so misdirecting, everyone forgot about the money and the peas. Without me even asking, people passed the Stars and Stripes top hat around and dropped money into it. I tried to give the beardy men their money back, but they said no, it had been worth it.

By the time Stars and Stripes got her hat back, it was nearly full of money. People seemed to think that because it was her hat, it must be her magic. And therefore her money. She didn't argue with this. She put the hat on her head with all the money inside it. Took a bow, collected all her Cups and Balls stuff, folded up her table, then said, 'You've been a wonderful audience. Please give my young helpers a round of applause!'

Nathan loved that. He kept bowing and smiling.

I was pretty pleased myself, being honest. The trick with the lunchbox had worked. People were surprised and amazed. And no one got hurt.

I mean *Ta-dah*! Or what?

I'd invented a trick. A trick I could swap with Perplexion if we ever managed to find him.

'We are wowing audiences,' said Nathan, smiling, 'in Las Vegas.'

'It was mostly Queenie,' said Brodie, 'being honest.'

But do you know what? You might think Stars and Stripes woman was being lovely, getting us a round of applause like that. Not like Perplexion.

Wrong.

That applause was just a sneaky piece of misdirection.

Because while we were standing there smiling and bowing and waving and loving it, Stars and Stripes strolled off with all the money.

She'd conned us.

It was Brodie who said it first. 'She's run off with all

the money,' he said. And ran after her.

Dodging in and out of that crowd was like swimming against the current of a giant wave machine, if the waves were wearing baseball hats and brightly coloured shirts. I thought we'd lost her, but Nathan shouted, 'The hat! Look! The hat!'

There was her top hat with its stars spangling away like a little ship on a sea of hats. She wasn't even running. I don't know what we thought we were going to do when we caught her. Call the police? Grab our money? Cry?

The one thing we didn't expect was that she would turn around, shout, 'Oh I love you kids! Group hug!' She threw her arms around us. 'And you, rabbit . . .'

'Queenie,' said Brodie.

'You've totally saved my life. That spot by the sign – that's supposed to be the best spot for street magic in the whole city, but I've never been able to make real money off it. People move off as soon as they've taken their selfie with the sign. So no one ever gives you money. That's why I ended up cheating people instead of doing real magic. You've brought real magic back into my life. I'll never do the con again. Thank you. Thank you. You know the greatest thing a magician can do is surprise another magician. And, boy, did you surprise me today. I saw that rabbit and I almost fainted. Good work. Really.'

She really did seem pleased with us. It seemed like she wanted to reward us. So I didn't feel shy about telling her that we needed help. I explained that we'd come to America by accident. 'We've got nothing,' I said.

'That's heartbreaking. I feel for you. I really do.' It really looked as if she was going to cry. 'Thoughts and prayers,' she said. And joined her hands in front of her.

I was pretty sure now that she really did want to help us. So I said, 'Instead of the thoughts and prayers, could you maybe give us some of that money?'

'Oh,' she said. 'Of course, go on, help yourselves.' She whipped off her hat and held it out to us. There was nothing in it.

Brodie said, 'There's nothing in it.'

She looked inside the hat and did a big surprised face. 'Oh!' she said. 'Magic! I guess the money did a vanishing act. Well isn't that just like money – vanishing when you most need it.'

'Magic,' I said, 'is supposed to make you feel wonder. This is just making me very, very disappointed.'

'Wait,' said Nathan, 'there IS something in there.' He reached in and pulled out a dull copper coin with a groove down the middle.

'Oh!' said Stars and Stripes. 'A lucky silver dollar! Lucky you!'

'It's not silver,' said Nathan.

'Honey,' she said, 'it's not a dollar either.'

The copper coin turned out to be a token. You buy them in the casino; then you put them in a slot machine, just like in the Lucky Star Arcade in Blackpool. It had the words *Valid for One Pull* written on one side and a picture of a bag full of money on the other.

'Go and see if it brings you luck,' she said. 'Luck is what this town is all about.'

'But we helped you get hundreds of dollars and you've got them all and all we get is this little token!? No thanks,' said Nathan, tucking it back in the hat.

'But you don't know what that is,' she said, 'until you put it in the machine. Maybe it's just another token, like you said. But maybe it's thirty-nine million dollars. That's what someone won with one of those things once, right here in this town. The machine paid out thirty-nine million dollars. Imagine that.'

Nathan gasped. 'How did they fit thirty-nine million dollars into one little slot machine?'

'Take yourselves over there,' she said, waving to a hotel across the road. 'Maybe you'll find out. Here. For you.' She put her top hat on Queenie's head.

CHAPTER TWENTY-THREE

WELCOME2CAMELOT

MIDDY:

We looked across the road at the hotel on the far side. I'm saying 'far side' because the other side of the road really was far away. Six lanes of thundering traffic away. But soaring up over the fumes and noise was a cluster of brightly coloured towers and turrets. It looked like the castle on the Disney logo. A big sign outside flashed the words *Welcome2Camelot*.

When we looked back, Stars and Stripes had gone. She'd managed to disappear by cleverly getting rid of her conspicuous hat before diving back into the crowd.

It didn't bother Nathan. 'Camelot,' he sighed. 'I've always want to see Camelot! And now here we are.'

'You do know,' I said, 'that that's not the real Camelot?'

'You say that about everything,' he said. 'You say magic isn't real. But here we are. Exactly like in my dream.'

'Oh, this is in your dream too?' I said. 'You didn't mention that Camelot was in your dream.'

'In my dream, we met Perplexion again. And now, in real life, he's just across the road. Look.'

Nathan was pointing at the electronic sign outside the Camelot Casino Hotel. The writing had disappeared from the sign and been replaced with a big, glowing face, staring at us across the road. It was the face of Perplexion, and written underneath that face were the words *Behold, Perplexion Is Here!*

Sometimes it seems life itself goes, *Ta–dah!*

BRODIE:

Nathan had this dream about him and Middy doing a massive magic show in Las Vegas with Perplexion. That dream was supposed to make us all feel better about being in Las Vegas when we were supposed to be home in time for tea.

Even if you believed in the dream, none of the really important things were in it. For instance:

How are we going to get home?

How are we going to contact Uncle Kevin and
    Auntie Anya (our phones didn't work)?

What are we going to eat?

What are we going to drink?

If we can't get home, where are we going to sleep?

Other things that were not mentioned in the dream:

Me . . .

Queenie!

Because the dream is all about the Wonder Brothers, and I'm not a Wonder Brother. And Queenie is a rabbit.

Well I'll tell you something, Captain Jimenez, if it wasn't for Queenie, The Wonder Brothers would still be standing under a palm tree waiting to cross the road in Las Vegas. Because that road was insane. A river of traffic. A man in bright blue shorts and a bright red shirt holding a big plastic goblet full of a bright yellow drink saw us standing there and asked us if we needed help to cross.

I said, 'Yes, please.'

He said, 'There's an old saying – the only way to get to the other side of this road is to be born there. Ha ha ha. Have a nice day.'

Well he didn't know Queenie. When Queenie wants to go somewhere, she goes. She does not take a detour. She slid out of my arms and sat up at the side of the road.

Queenie was still wearing the spangly top hat.

A giant rabbit in a spangly top hat – any driver is

going to slow down to look at a sight like that. And when the first car slowed down, she bounced into the road. The car slammed on its brakes. Its driver pounded on her horn. Queenie trotted across the lane without even looking. The driver in the next lane saw her coming and slammed on her brakes too. More car horns. More screeches of brakes. Basically Queenie created an instant pedestrian crossing. She led us across the road like a rabbit traffic warden. She didn't even seem to notice the honking horns and waving fists.

'Pretty drastic,' said Middy. 'She could have used a lollipop.'

CHAPTER TWENTY-FOUR

HALL OF FORTUNE

NATHAN:

Everything in the Camelot Casino Hotel is to do with King Arthur. The entrance is a drawbridge over an artificial moat. There's a little mechanical dragon called Lucy. She guards the gate. And blows smoke at you and says, '*Camelot welcomes careful gamblers.*' There's a boat shaped like a swan drifting around the moat. When you get to the middle of the bridge, a big bell rings out and mysterious mists spread across the waters. A woman's arm rises from the depths holding a beautiful sword. Then the arm sinks down into the water again and the mist blows away.

'Can you believe this?' I said. 'The Lady of the Lake is staying in this hotel!'

Middy said it was probably just her arm. Brodie got very excited because he'd seen a sign saying *Free Wi-Fi*.

I said, 'Brodie, why would anyone think about

Wi-Fi when there's an underwater lady waving swords around in a magical mist?'

Brodie said that if he could get on the Wi-Fi, he would WhatsApp uncle Kevin and tell him we were safe and ask him to book us some flights home.

'He's not going to enjoy hearing we're in Las Vegas,' said Middy. 'He did tell us to be home in time for tea.'

To be honest, I was beginning to think about home too. I think it was the smell again. They have little wooden kiosks all across the bridge. Like in a medieval fair. But selling hot dogs and tacos and burgers and ice cream instead of, I don't know, pigs' heads and magic potions. The point is it smelled like Blackpool. It also smelled of food. This reminded me that I was starving.

I went through my bag looking for a phone charger, but it was entirely full of magic stuff. Cups, balls, cards, baby wipes, string and coins for vanishing. I had the flag of Cambodia. But I didn't have a phone charger. Brodie didn't have a bag at all, just a pocket full of spare carrots for his rabbit.

And Middy's bag was nearly entirely full of her Exploding Lunchbox trick. In other words, a plastic box full of smaller plastic boxes.

Brodie said he was too hungry to keep on breathing that air. But Middy didn't seem even a little bit worried, or tired, or hungry. She was just looking at the door of the hotel as though it was the starting line of a race – a race she was going to win.

'When I've shown him my trick,' she said, 'Perplexion will phone home for us.'

I said, 'You can't ask the world's greatest magician to phone your dad.'

She said, 'You can if you're going to show him a trick he can't do.'

'How do you know he can't do it?' I said.

Middy smiled. 'For hundreds of years, people have been trying to do the Exploding Box without knocking themselves senseless. I'm the first one to figure out how to do it. When he sees that, he'll want us to be friends. Trust me.'

Middy strode towards Camelot. The great big automatic wooden doors swung open as though some invisible lord was welcoming her in like a visiting queen.

Then there we were, in this vast room, with shields and swords on the walls and rafters over your head. It's called the Hall of Fortune, because instead of kings and queens and courtiers, there are rows and rows of slot machines. To be fair, the slot machines do look a bit like knights in armour, being made of metal and each one waving one hand in the air like a salute. If there was a magic land called SlotMachinia, this is what its army would look like.

I said, 'Let's give our lucky dollar a spin.'

But – guess what – all the machines in there are contactless! They don't take coins.

The people who worked for the hotel all wore suits of armour with their names written on them. We found one whose badge said *Knight of Welcome* and asked him if there was anywhere we could spend our token.

'We do not operate machines with coins, my lord,' he said. 'Know ye not, all the casinos hereabout prefer contactless. For lo, it lets you spend more gold more quickly.'

'That's nice,' said Brodie.

Middy said it was just the same in the Lucky Star Arcade back home. She didn't want to give the impression that Las Vegas was better than Blackpool. 'Besides,' she said. 'We're not here to gamble.'

'You're not allowed to anyway,' said the Knight of Welcome. 'You're too young. Also, please keep moving. Children are allowed to pass through the Hall of Fortune, but not to stand still.'

'We are here,' said Middy, 'to see Perplexion.'

'Yonder lies the fully air-conditioned Camelot Theatre and Hotel,' said the Knight of Welcome. 'Please keep moving.' He pointed us towards a flashing sign at the far end of the hall.

Dreams Are Made, it said, *This Way*.

'Let's go,' said Middy.

The sign pointed to a golden door. Middy stood in front of it for a moment. I nearly always know what she's feeling. She was feeling nervous.

'Come on,' I said. 'All you have to do is trust the dream.'

And we went through the golden door.

CHAPTER TWENTY-FIVE

VIP SPA DAY – *BABY!*

MIDDY:

You only get one chance with magic. As Karabas says in *My Secrets Revealed* (page fifty).

> *With magic, you only get one chance. Do a trick badly the first time and it doesn't matter how brilliantly you do it the second time – it won't be magic. Do not perform unless you're feeling perfect.*

I wasn't feeling perfect. My stomach was the size of a golf ball. A family walking by gave us funny looks, which reminded me that we'd slept in our spangly clothes. And the last time we'd washed or brushed our teeth was on the other side of the Atlantic Ocean.

'Nathan,' I said, 'I think we smell. We can't see Perplexion looking like this. We'll only get one chance. We have to give it our best shot.'

'OK,' said Nathan. 'Let me think.'

If I'd been doing the thinking, I would have thought, *Let's find some toilets and freshen up*. But Nathan thinks bigger.

There's a massive stone fireplace in the entrance to the hotel. There's antlers on the wall over the mantelpiece and logs blazing away in the grate, which is big enough to roast a pig in. It's not a real fire, obviously. But it looks good. Next to it is a great big poster that looks like an ancient treasure map, pinned to the wall with arrows, but it's actually a diagram of the hotel. Brodie was studying away at that.

'I did not enjoy being stuck in that truck,' Brodie said, looking at the map. 'From now on, wherever I go, I'm going to locate and memorize all the exits.'

Nathan looked at the map too. Then he said, 'Right. Let's go. We're off to the very top.'

The lifts are cute, by the way. There's a pair of battleaxes blocking the entrance. When the doors open, the battleaxes lift up to let you pass. We took the lift to the fortieth floor. Forty floors! When you come out of the lift, the place is lit by floaty candles, like in *Harry Potter*, except they're electric candles not real ones. There's music playing that sounds like faraway monks singing.

Across the way is a big glass door with the words *Lady of the Lake Luxury Spa* engraved on it and a picture of an arm holding a sword. Nathan made us sit on a little bench shaped like a crouching lion. We waited there until a man and woman came by, chatting to each other. She was carrying a big towel covered in pictures of cactuses. He had a shiny bald head. He waved a plastic card at the glass door and it opened.

'Now,' said Nathan. 'Walk normal. And keep that rabbit out of sight.'

We strolled after the couple and through the glass doors just as they were closing, into the cleanest, brightest place I'd ever seen. White tiles on the floor and walls. Gleaming mirrors. People in glowy white overalls with even whiter smiles. Honestly, just walking in made me feel spruce.

The woman at the desk said, 'Welcome to the Lady of the Lake Luxury VIP Spa. Room number, please?' Then she turned her smile on and it was blinding.

Nathan said, 'Oh . . .' and looked across at the two people who went in just ahead of us – Cactus Towel Woman and Shiny-Head Guy. They were busy taking selfies with the Camelot coat of arms in the background.

The woman said, 'VIP spa day, *baby!*' into her phone. The man made her say it again because his head was too shiny in the picture.

Nathan didn't exactly say anything, but the way he looked at them definitely gave the smiley woman the idea that they were our mum and dad.

'Oh, I'm so sorry,' she blustered. 'Such a pleasure to meet our Camelot Junior VIP Club members. Here are your Junior VIP goody bags. And I guess you know your way to the changing rooms. I'm Lady Eleanor, and I'll be your respectful servant today.' Lady Eleanor gave us towels that looked like little piles of fluffy white clouds.

I highly recommend Camelot Junior VIP Club goody bags. Mine had a swimming costume and cap, a bar of lovely soap, a pair of flip-flops and some sun cream, all with the Camelot VIP Club coat of arms on them. Being honest, the best thing of all was a complimentary toothbrush-and-toothpaste set. I drenched myself in the shower, scrubbed my teeth, and then . . .

Oh my days, the Camelot Casino Hotel outdoor pool is five star. It's on the roof! Forty floors up! You're hundreds of feet in the air, swimming under a blue sky, with palm branches waving over you. It feels like flying. The pool goes right to the edge on one side. There's a glass wall to keep you safe but still give you the view. You could see the pretend Eiffel Tower, and the towers of the other hotels, and beyond them the desert, the mountains and more mountains.

I said, 'Woah.'

Brodie said, 'It looks like Blackpool but with the tide out.'

Nathan said, 'You know I get the feeling this is the kind of place they give you food.'

As soon as he said this, we realized we were starving. We climbed out of the pool and parked ourselves on the sun loungers opposite a TV screen the size of a tennis court. There was a pile of menus printed on parchment with little paintings of the food next to the names and prices. I was already hungry enough. Just looking at those pictures made me nearly die of starvation.

Nathan was very interested in corn dogs because he'd heard of them but never had one. I felt the same about Pop Tarts.

Lady Eleanor saw us looking at the menus and came over to take our order. 'My lords – and lady, of course – what can we get you this merry afternoon?'

She never said anything about money or paying, so we asked for three Flagons of Soda, three Ye Olde Beef Burgers and three Goodly Portions of Fries. We'd decided against corn dogs and Pop Tarts because this was definitely not the time to try something new. Brodie was worried that Queenie wouldn't like any of these, so we added a side salad.

Lady Eleanor told us that we'd hear a fanfare from the pavilion when the order was ready. And we did! An actual fanfare played on an actual trumpet by a man wearing a pair of bright yellow trousers and a hat with a feather in it. It came from the little stripy tent

– the pavilion – at the far end of the pool. When he'd finished playing, Lady Eleanor brought the food over.

When you see someone off the telly in real life – like at the Big Switch-On in Blackpool – they always look smaller than in the pictures. In America, when you see food in real life, it always looks bigger than in the pictures. Queenie's side salad was the size of a garden centre.

'Look at all this,' sighed Nathan. 'Trust the dream, or what?'

Lady Eleanor was about to hand all this over when Brodie said, 'We're on telly, by the way.'

As usual he didn't use an exclamation mark, but that didn't matter because Lady Eleanor used up probably every single exclamation mark in the World when she said, 'You are!!!!!! You're on TV !!!!!!!!!!!!!!!!!!!!!!!!!!!' She nearly dropped the tray of food.

People had filmed Middy doing her magic act by

the *Welcome to Las Vegas* sign, and for some reason this was now on the news. We couldn't hear what they were saying about us because the sound was off. There was a strip along the bottom of the massive screen saying, *Brit kids wow crowds,* which sounded good. And they were showing a clip of Queenie appearing from out of a lunchbox that was much smaller than she was.

I went for one of the burgers, but Lady Eleanor turned away to tell the man with the shiny head that we were on TV. 'They're on TV!' She whooped, moving the burger just out of my reach.

The man glanced at the screen, then at us. Then he said, 'That's nice,' and swam off.

'Nice?!' said Lady Eleanor. 'It's AWESOME. Awesomely awesome.' She was bouncing up and down.

I had forgotten until then that she thought these people were our parents. The direction this conversation was taking was worrying, but not as worrying as the possibility that those burgers might end up in the water.

So I said, 'I'm not sure that's us. I think it's someone who looks a bit like us, but . . . shall I take the fries?'

'Oh sure,' she replied.

But just as I got my hands to them, Queenie's head popped out of Nathan's backpack and looked around.

'Oh! I see the rabbit is poolside too!' said Lady Eleanor, and she gave Cactus Towel Woman a really stern look. 'You know,' she said, 'pets are strictly forbidden from entering the Lady of the Lake Spa.'

'OK.' Cactus Towel Woman shrugged, looking a bit confused.

'Though I suppose if your pet can appear and disappear like magic,' Lady Eleanor continued, 'there's nothing you can do to stop it!!!!!!'

'No.' Cactus Towel Woman was now nervously backing away with the towel in front of her.

Lady Eleanor said she loved magic and asked them

if they'd managed to get Perplexion tickets.

'Yes.' Cactus Towel Woman was clutching the towel really tight now and looking around for some sign of Shiny-Head guy. 'Thank you. We have tickets.'

'No, we haven't got tickets,' said Nathan, 'or burgers yet.'

He reached for one.

'That's a shame. I mean, I know those tickets are very expensive . . .'

'Two thousand dollars each,' said Shiny-Head Guy, his head popping up out of the water like a seal. 'But then they are ringside seats for History itself.'

'Perplexion's last ever show! Every famous magician in the world is going to be there to see his last show. David Blaine. David Copperfield. Chris Pilsworth. Chris Ramsay. You name them. It's a crying pity your kids can't go too,' said Lady Eleanor. 'Especially with them being such awesome magicians themselves.'

Nathan had finally got a finger to one of the burgers when Cactus Towel Woman said, 'But they're not OUR kids.'

Lady Eleanor whipped the tray out of reach again. 'Not your . . . ? But whose are they? I mean who is paying for these?' She brandished the tray of food at them.

It was time for emergency magic skills.

Nathan pointed to the middle of the pool.

'What's that?' he said.

I mean, that is the most basic misdirection you could ever do, but it does work. Lady Eleanor looked away and Nathan palmed one burger. I stood behind him and took it while he swiped the fries.

Then I saw that this wasn't just misdirection. Something really *was* happening in the pool. The water was gathering itself into a boiling dome shape, as though some huge creature was rising from the depths.

'Is that a wave machine?' said Brodie.

'Everyone out of the water. Right away,' said Lady Eleanor, though everyone was clambering out of the water already.

The dome of water broke into a wave that roared off up and down the pool.

'Nothing to worry about,' announced Lady Eleanor to all the guests. 'This is not a quake. It's just a mild earth tremor. You are in no present danger. However, we do ask club members to leave the rooftop until until Camelot has stopped shaking.'

Then she turned back to us. But we were gone.

We're magicians.

We do know how to vanish.

CHAPTER TWENTY-SIX

GREAT MAGICIANS OF HISTORY

NATHAN:

I mean . . . Come. On. I said trust the dream, didn't I? Even I didn't expect the actual earth to actually shake just so we could get free burgers and fries. I know Vegas gets a lot of earth tremors. They happen all the time. But not at absolutely exactly the right time for free food.

Wonders!

We grabbed our clothes from the changing room. We ate the food on the stairs. The hotel had stopped swaying. We were fresh, fed and ready to meet Perplexion.

Brodie said, 'If he's in the theatre, there are two main entrances on the ground floor. There are also fire exits that you can get to from the back stairs, and also the backstage area opens directly onto the grassy area at the side of the moat. That's so they can get big props on and off the stage.'

He really had studied that map.

MIDDY:

There are only so many ways to astound people. You can make things appear, make them disappear, make them float in the air. You can make people think you can read their minds. You can change things (for instance handkerchiefs) into other things (for instance doves). The magician's job is to make those old tricks seem to be new and wonderful. How do you do that? You take something old and you add . . . you. You are unique and amazing. If you give your unique and amazing self to your trick, it will be unique and amazing too.

Karabas the Modest, *My Secrets Revealed*

That's exactly what I'd done, wasn't it, with my Exploding Lunchbox?

I'd taken a trick that was invented two hundred years ago and I'd added me to it. De Kolta's box was made of metal and covered in magical symbols.

In the old version, something that looked magical turned out to be magical. Well, what did you expect?

In my version, a regular school lunchbox turned out to be magical. No one is expecting that! A rabbit in a lunchbox?!

152

Ta-dah!

We had a great trick.

We had appeared on American TV (I know, I know, we didn't actually know what they'd said about us because the volume was turned down).

We were ready.

There was no need to be nervous.

But I was nervous.

Nervous all the way along the corridor that led to the theatre entrance. All along the walls there were scenes from magic history.

There was a photograph of Houdini tied up in chains.

A painting of Ching Ling Foo in his silken robes with his beheading sword.

A cartoon of Richard Potter cooking a pancake on his top hat.

A photograph of Lulu Hurst performing her supernatural feat of strength by lifting up two huge blokes.

There was a screen showing film of Fay Presto making a bottle travel through a table.

Another screen showing film of David Copperfield flying all around the theatre . . .

The thing is, every magician, in every one of those pictures, seemed to be looking down at me and laughing to themselves.

How could we possibly ever have imagined that the Wonder Brothers could do magic like these people?

The worst was a photo of De Kolta himself with his Exploding Box. He looked like a proper magician with his curling moustache and his glossy top hat. And here I was claiming that I'd taken that man's most famous trick and made it better.

No, that wasn't the worst really. The very worst was the really big screen showing Perplexion walking through a plate-glass window without breaking it. He didn't even look human. More like a ghost or an angel. At the end of the clip the title of the show came up – 'Dreams Are Made' – and then it said, 'Last Chance to See'.

Sitting at the entrance, in front of a thick red curtain, a woman dressed like Maid Marian was scrolling through her phone. When she saw us, she said, 'Pray, how may I help thee?'

I meant to say, 'We'd like to see Perplexion,' but it came out as, 'We're ready to see Perplexion.'

'Verily,' she said. 'But Perplexion doth not want to see thee. Not until eight of the clock, and only then if ye haveth tickets.'

Brodie told her we didn't have tickets.

'Then you cannot see him at all. For, know ye not, there is no admission without tickets.'

Nathan said, 'We don't want to see his show. We

154

want to see him. We want to show him something.'

I said, 'He'll really like it.'

'Look, kid,' said Maid Marian, suddenly sounding a bit less medieval. 'The man's rehearsing. He's not going to see anyone. This is his last show. It's a big deal. Every famous magician in the world is here. Do you know who I saw earlier in the hotel barber shop? David actual Copperfield, that's who. He's come to see the show. With a new haircut. I don't know who you are, but unless you're more important than the actual David actual Copperfield, move on.'

I said it would only take a minute. 'Couldn't you sneak us in for just one minute?'

She pulled the curtain back. There was a big metal grid with spikes on the end. 'It's called a portcullis,' she said. 'No one is getting past that. Not without a ticket. Go and buy one. You can get one for a couple of thousand dollars. Until then, if you don't mind, I was in the middle of a game of chess.' She took her phone out again.

My heart was sinking.

Then Nathan said, 'I don't think we've explained properly. We've got something he wants.' And out of his pocket, he took Perplexion's watch. 'Here. See. His name is engraved there. We think he'd probably like it back.'

'Oh. Thanks. I'll see that he gets it,' said the

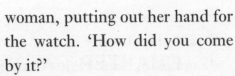

woman, putting out her hand for the watch. 'How did you come by it?'

'I think we'd rather see that he gets it ourselves,' said Nathan, putting the watch back in his pocket. 'We've come a long way.'

She looked at the watch. Then she glanced at Nathan. 'Do I know you from somewhere? I feel like I've seen you somewhere recently.'

I was going to say, 'Maybe you saw us on TV . . .' but she said, 'No, it's not you. That cape. I know that cape. That's Perplexion's cape. Do you have any more of his stuff? What did you do? Ransack his dressing room?'

'No . . . I . . .'

'Wait here,' she said, ducking under the curtain. 'I'll be right back.'

I hissed at Nathan, 'We gave him his watch back in Blackpool. I gave it to him myself.'

Nathan shrugged, 'Stole it back.'

'What?! Why?'

'Practice.'

CHAPTER TWENTY-SEVEN

MEGABUCKS

BRODIE:

Middy and Nathan were interested in the pictures of old-time magicians. Queenie wasn't. She was interested in an exhibition of old-style casino equipment. She went bobbing off down the corridor, twitching her nose at all the old fruit machines, slot machines and arcade games.

I had no money. We only had the Stars and Stripes woman's lucky dollar – which wasn't a dollar, and could not be used in modern machines, so it wasn't very lucky either.

But the slot machine that Queenie was staring at wasn't modern. It was so old, it had a plaque next to it saying, *It was on this machine that in 2003 Mrs Elvira Anonymous – after spending less than $10 – won $39,000,000, the biggest jackpot of all time.*

There was a man staring at it already. 'This is the very slot machine . . .' he said. Then he paused to take a drink from this absolute bucket of purple slushy he was carrying. 'The very slot machine,' he said again, before taking another gulp. 'On which some lucky woman –' gulp – 'won –' gulp – 'thirty-nine million dollars in 2003.'

'I know,' I said. 'It says so on the plaque on the wall.'

'What is not recorded –' gulp – 'is that she was a sight even luckier than you might think.'

I could tell he really, really wanted me to ask why. But just then a woman came along, fanning herself with a hat the size of a wagon wheel. She kissed the man on the cheek. 'I knew I'd find you here,' she said. 'Has Leon been telling you his sob story?'

Leon said it wasn't really a sob story. 'The day that woman won, my dad was the very next in line to play,' he said. 'Can you imagine? If the woman who won had stepped away just one pull earlier, I'd've been raised by a multi-millionaire.'

'And you'd never have met me,' said the woman.

'That is a true word.' Leon smiled. 'Luckiest break of my life – my dad being doomed to a life of hard work and low wages.'

The woman slipped her arm around Leon's waist.

I had the lucky dollar in my pocket. Surely it would be worth trying to win some money. I might even win enough to buy plane tickets home.

I went to drop the token into the slot. But someone stopped me.

'Whoah!' shouted a woman who was shimmying out of the lift in a shimmery dress. She had shoes with dagger heels that she was carrying in her hand. On her feet she had a pair of trainers.

'Honey,' she said, 'you're not allowed to play the machines if you're under twenty-one. You'll have to ask someone else to play it for you. Imagine that. Imagine if you won. You wouldn't be allowed to touch the money because you're underage.'

I said, 'Phew. That would've been unlucky.'

'You don't know what unlucky is, sweetie,' she said. 'Not unless you're me.'

Like the man with the slushy, she really wanted me to ask her why. Apparently, she told us, on her twenty-first birthday she was in the Hall of Fortune queuing to play this very machine. It's called the Mega Bucks.

'I was next in the queue – the very next,' she said. 'Had my birthday money in my hand – when suddenly this machine paid out that thirty-nine million dollars. Imagine that. I was one pull away from being a multi-millionaire. I've never played the slots since. You really don't want to ask me to play it for you.'

She waved her shoes at a cluster of women who were waiting at the far end of the corridor. They all waved their shoes back and called her over.

As she moved away she nearly bumped into an old man with long white hair and a cowboy hat. His cowboy hat hit the floor, and he would've too if I hadn't grabbed him by the elbow and steadied him.

'My thanks to you, young sir,' he said. 'That woman was going like a tornado. Now if you pass my hat, I'll wish you good day and be on my way.'

I gave him his hat. He looked at the slot machine and sighed, 'Thirty-nine million dollars.'

'You must have been so disappointed,' I said.

He looked at me. 'Me? Disappointed? Why?'

'Weren't you next in the queue when the woman won all that money. Nearly everyone else round here was apparently. Just one pull away from being a millionaire.'

'Me?' he said. 'Not me. No. I wasn't next in the queue . . .'

'Oh. I was beginning to think that everyone in Las Vegas was in that queue.'

'I wasn't next in the queue, I was the one *before* her in the queue. I put my last dollar in that machine. My very last dollar. Then I walked off and she put her first dollar in it. I looked back just in time to see her whole life change in a shower of shiny tokens. I'll never forget it. If I'd had just one more token.'

I told him I had a spare one. If he wanted to use it, we could split the winnings. 'I'm too young to use it myself,' I added.

I held out my hand. He stared at the token.

160

'No,' he said. 'That could be your lucky token. You don't want to hand that over to the unluckiest man alive.' He took his hat and strolled off. 'Please don't tell me how you did,' he called over his shoulder. 'Because I don't want to know.'

A voice behind me said, 'Well what do we have here?' The voice was thick like chip shop gravy. In the glass of the slot machine I could see a face like a skull with sunglasses like eye sockets. There was a splash of red hair. It was the reflection of Perplexion's bodyguard. He was standing behind mc. I looked down the corridor, thinking Perplexion must be coming. He wasn't. But his glamorous assistant, Zenith was. And she had a police officer with her. They were heading for Nathan and Middy.

The bodyguard didn't say a thing. He wouldn't know it was me, I realized, so long as I didn't turn around. I needed to buy some time, so I said the first thing I could think of, which was, 'I'm too young to play. But what if you put the coin in and I pulled the handle?'

'Sure.' His voice buzzed the hairs on the back of my neck.

I passed the coin back to him and stood ready by the handle. He dropped the coin in the slot. I pulled the handle.

The Mega Bucks sign flashed right in our eyes. Then

the machine made a noise. Lights danced all across its screen. It stopped. Went quiet. And a tumble of gold coins came crashing out all over the floor. The words BIG WIN flashed up on the screen.

The bodyguard just stared at the screen.

I bent down to pick up the coins.

But that's when Nathan and Middy came tearing past me, telling me to 'Run!'

So I scooped up Queenie from where she'd been hiding and ran.

CHAPTER TWENTY-EIGHT

THE ENCHANTED BOAT

CAPTAIN JIMENEZ:

I asked Sergeant Jamie to check the Camelot Casino Hotel lobby CCTV – we saw them marching in, bold as you please, but there was no recording of them leaving. There was nothing. Nothing. Nada.

Stating for the record: The children were finally recorded on CCTV riding the Loop downtown towards Fremont. They then vanished again.

I asked Sergeant Jamie how come these children can move around the city undetected.

Sergeant Jamie said, 'They just seem to be able to disappear, ma'am.'

I responded, 'How can three children disappear? They're not exactly inconspicuous. One of them is wearing a bejewelled cape. Another one is carrying a rabbit the size of a pig.'

Sergeant Jamie suggested, 'Magic?'

I terminated the conversation.

NATHAN:

No. But listen. How we got out of that hotel. That was definitely magic.

We were waiting by the curtain. Middy was standing there, saying nothing, getting herself into the magic zone, waiting for the moment that Perplexion would come and behold the magic of the Wonder Brothers. Then she growled at me out of the corner of her mouth, 'Why are you still wearing his cape?'

'I like it.'

'Take it off.'

'But it's got all these secret pockets.'

'Take it off. Fold it up and the minute he comes through that curtain, hand it back to him with a big smile.'

The curtain twitched. Middy grabbed my hand for a second, thinking – this is it. This is what we came all this way for. Perplexion.

It wasn't Perplexion.

It was Zenith. She wore her hair tied back and had the look of someone who's just been interrupted while they're doing something important.

'I hear,' she said, 'you found the big guy's watch. Thank you. It was very important to him. Here's a couple of signed photographs as a thank you. And fifty dollars.'

'Oh, we don't want money,' said Middy, a bit too quickly in my opinion. 'We just want to see him.'

'Buy a ticket,' Zenith said.

I laughed. I probably shouldn't have done that, but *come on*. Two thousand dollars for one ticket!

Zenith gave me a look that would freeze fireworks and said, 'Where's the watch?'

'We wanted to show him something,' said Middy. Her voice was a bit squeaky. 'We've come a long way. We've sort of followed him here from Blackpool. We've got a trick. A new one. He'll love it.'

'I highly doubt that,' said Zenith. Her pencilled-on eyebrows scribbled a frown on her face.

Middy held up her Exploding Lunchbox. 'It's . . .'

But before she could say any more, Zenith took the lunchbox out of her hand, spun it round a few times on her finger tips and held it up to the light. 'De Kolta's box,' she said. 'This trick is hundreds of years old.'

Middy nodded. 'Yes, but I've improved it.'

'You were on TV!' said Zenith. 'You did this with a rabbit.' She had changed her tone. A little bit of a smile began to turn up the corners of her mouth. Middy began to smile too. Zenith looked her in the eyes and started talking more quietly.

'Every night on Perplexion's show,' Zenith said, 'just after the interval I ask if there's anyone in the audience who thinks they can surprise Perplexion. People come up and do their tricks, and every single time, without saying a word, Perplexion does the same trick straight after them. He can always see how it's done. He's got nothing to learn. A magician who can't be surprised. That's a sad thing. It's time for him to stop.'

Middy was really listening to this. But I'd seen people talk like this before. Zenith was talking like a magician. She was misdirecting Middy. And Middy was acting like a volunteer from the audience.

Something was going on.

I looked down the corridor and noticed Mr Steak Bake bodyguard standing right behind Brodie.

When Zenith said, 'Just wait here one minute,' and slipped behind the curtain, I knew that whatever she was going to get from behind the curtain, it was not going to be Perplexion.

Further along the corridor there was a glass door that led out onto a terrace. I could see the Maid Marian woman talking to a hotel security guy – he looked like a wrestler. Mr Wrestler glanced towards us through the door. Next thing, Zenith joined them.

Middy didn't notice any of this. She was still looking at the gap in the curtain, waiting for Perplexion to swish through.

She was still thinking like a volunteer from the audience.

I was still thinking like a magician – noticing everything. I noticed for instance, that Zenith had taken Middy's lunchbox. And I noticed that Zenith had gone off in one direction and Maid Marian in the other. I especially noticed that Mr Wrestler took out his walkie-talkie.

They were going to surround us.

Like I said, Middy sometimes worries I'm going to say the wrong thing.

This time I said the right thing. I said, 'Run!'

And we ran.

BRODIE

I'm trying to remember the order things happened. Mr Steak Bake pulled the handle of the slot machine. The screen went crazy with flashing patterns of fruit and bells. Then it all stopped. There was a really, really bright flash, like a photograph being taken. Then there was the sound of gold tokens pouring out of the front of the machine. So just then, all I was thinking was, *I've won!*

The next thing, Nathan was tugging at my jacket and Middy was yelling, 'Run! Run!'

Mr Steak Bake shouted, 'Stop! Stop them!' Which only made me run faster.

We got back to the main entrance with the huge fireplace and the antlers. It was busy. People heading for the restaurants, coming back from the gym, going to the casino, collecting their kids from the play centre. Nearly all these people looked round when Mr Steak Bake shouted stop.

Even Middy and Nathan stopped and looked around, not knowing which way to go. But here's where my specialist knowledge of hotel geography kicked in.

'This way,' I said, and took them down the emergency stairs behind the lifts. That staircase is the recommended route out of the building in case of fire. There should definitely be more signs pointing to it. Good thing for us that there weren't.

I barged through that door. Down two more flights of stairs and along a narrow tunnel type thing, then through a door marked *Authorized Only*.

It was pitch dark.

We let the door close quietly behind us.

Middy said, 'Where are we?'

'In the dark,' said Nathan.

I thought we were under the stage area. To be honest, I was surprised it was so dark. Nathan shoved us forward.

'Rabbits can see in the dark,' he said. 'Queenie can lead us.'

But the minute we took one step into the shadows, light exploded all around us. Strange shadows flew up the walls. And there was the big wooden pharaoh looking down at us. We were definitely under the stage.

I looked back thinking someone had come in after us and turned the lights on. But the lights were the kind that switch on automatically if someone comes in.

'What exactly,' said Middy, 'are we running away from?'

Nathan said, 'Trouble.'

Being honest, Nathan does know a LOT about trouble. He definitely knows when it's coming. According to the map, the nearest exit was straight ahead.

'Not sure,' I said, 'but I think this is where they bring in the big props.'

The props were all around us. It was just like being back in the truck. There was a big black metal piece of kit in the middle of the floor. It was a kind of platform sitting on a bunch of big cogs with wires and chains sticking out of it.

Middy said it was probably the lift to the trapdoor. For disappearing things. 'It must lead to the stage. Couldn't we just, you know, sneak up for a minute. He might be . . .'

As soon as she said that, we heard the door bang open behind us and a voice that sounded like hot gravy poured through the room. 'They must be in here. Flush them out and I'll . . .'

No one wanted to hear the rest of the sentence.

We were through that exit and outside in moments.

Exactly like on the map, we were on the little green bit by the moat. I felt slightly chuffed with my map-reading skills.

Then Middy said, 'There's a barbed wire fence on one side of us. There's a fake waterfall with an electric rainbow on the other. There's the moat in front of us. And Mr Steak Bake behind us. What are we going to do? Swim?'

NATHAN:

This is my point. We were trapped. I mean completely trapped. Then what happened?

There was a buzzing sound. Then the electric rainbow lit up and invisible hunting horns played a sad-sounding call. Then, out from under the waterfall came . . . a boat!

An actual boat, shaped like a swan with King Arthur sitting in the back looking royal.

I mean, the boat was an actual boat, but it was not the actual King Arthur. He was just a kind of waxwork figure with an arm that goes up and down waving a sword around.

It was the boat that floats across the moat every couple of hours to collect the sword from the Lady of the Lake.

I said, 'Quick! Get on board!'

The others hesitated. The boat didn't look like it could carry all of us. Also, Middy said, 'Do you really think people aren't going to notice three kids and a rabbit bobbing along on a magical medieval water feature? Nathan, you are such a muffin sometimes.'

'Am I though? Am I really? Because look . . .'

I pointed to the moat. A mystical mist had spread across its surface. If we lay down in the boat, the swan's wings would cover us completely. We dived in. And next thing, we are racketing off down the ramp like a log flume at the court of King Arthur. *Splash!* We hit the water and go floating across the moat.

When we looked back we could see the massive shape of Mr Steak Bake looming from the clouds, looking for us, but we were gone.

VANISHED!

We drifted along until the swan ground to a halt under the bridge. Then we stepped out onto a little walkway and strolled up the ramp. Looking back towards the Camelot Casino Hotel, what do we see?

Zenith in her long red coat, standing at the main entrance, and next to her – a police car. She's talking to the police. She called the police on us!

'She said she was going to get Perplexion,' Middy squeaked, 'and then she called the police on us! Why?! What did we ever do to her?!'

Brodie said, 'Well, I don't think we're supposed to be in the country without passports. And I definitely think we're not supposed to be lounging around a hotel spa eating VIP burgers.'

'We were so near,' wailed Middy. 'We were nearly in the same room as him.'

But that's not the point. The point is at the exact moment we were nearly caught, who comes along to rescue us? Only King Arthur in a boat, that's all.

See what I mean?

Trust. The. Dream.

CHAPTER TWENTY-NINE

IT'S A DANGEROUS PLACE, KIDDO

CAPTAIN JIMENEZ:

If you think leaving a theatre by means of
the back door is magic, I can assure you
it's not. Yeah, you kids did vamoose from the Camelot
Casino Hotel, but you certainly did not vanish.

Thanks to the good work of Sergeant Jamie we, here
at Operation Tower, have in our possession CCTV
footage of you riding around on the Loop. I will now
show this for the purposes of identification.

For the record, the boy Nathan said, 'It's us! On
TV!!'

The girl, Middy, said, 'That Loop bus was so cool.
I mean literally. It had air conditioning.'

The other boy, Brodie, said, 'And it was free! I
thought we could ride around on that all night, but the
driver spotted Queenie and said no animals allowed.
We had to get off in Freedom.'

'Freedom?'

'It's a place with loads of arcades and cafes and . . .' Brodie replied.

'Fremont. Not Freedom.'

I explained that the place was called Fremont, and that it has more than its fair share of highly spiced characters.

I also explained that despite its reputation for law-breakers and misfits, the people there were alarmed and horrified to see three children walking around the place without any apparent adult supervision. One concerned citizen uploaded this film to our social media feed, where Sergeant Jamie here found it.

I will now play the film so as to remove all doubt and insinuation.

'Why did they do that?' asked the boy Brodie. 'Why did they give the film to the police?'

'The lady was worried about you,' said Sergeant Jamie. 'It's a dangerous place, kiddo.'

The girl Middy said, 'She fed Queenie the salad from her burger.'

'Missy,' I said, 'I've interviewed enough frauds and tricksters in my life to know when I'm being led away from the river and into the trees. I will not be distracted by rabbit chit-chat.'

As for 'Trusting the Dream', look at where you are. You are in police custody. No one is going to let you leave here in order to gatecrash a one-night-only world–exclusive farewell performance of probably the finest magician in Vegas. So that part of your dream isn't happening. Plus you don't have a magic trick of your own since Zenith confiscated your lunchbox trick.

I may have made this point too forcefully. The girl Middy began to cry.

'We are not living Nathan's dream at all,' she said. 'We'll never get to the show. We've got no money. Everything seemed to be going so well. We thought we were going to see him. We thought we were going to fix everything. And now . . .'

Sergeant Jamie was now crying also.

I told him to shape up.

'Sergeant,' I said. 'They are in the country without the proper papers. They have stowed away illegally on an aircraft. They have stolen food, swimming costumes, flip-flops and a valuable timepiece belonging to . . .'

Then the boy Nathan stood up and said, 'These are just details. Middy DOES have a great trick. A new one. It just came to her in Fremont.'

CHAPTER THIRTY

ZOMBIE WEDDING

MIDDY:

You don't make magic. You find it.

Karabas the Modest, *My Secrets Revealed*

This is so true. That trick just dropped into my hands like prize money dropping out of a slot machine.

All the time I'd been trying to think of ways to impress Perplexion, I'd been thinking of tricks that were like Perplexion tricks. Big illusion tricks with special props, like ancient sarcophaguses and amazing music and lights. Silvery-pants type tricks.

I had nothing. Zenith had repossessed my De Kolta lunchbox.

But I found magic in Fremont.

Or maybe it found me.

This is how it happened.

We got off the Loop bus outside a building that looked like one big tombstone. I don't think it was made of real stone. Carved on the front in tall, serious-looking letters, it said, *Till Death Doth Us Part*.

The other two didn't like the look of it, but I showed them the bit on page forty seven of *My Secrets Revealed* where Karabas says, '*Magic is a campfire. Light it and people will be drawn to its glow.*'

'I'm not sure,' said Brodie, 'that I want to share a campfire with those people.' He nodded to the queue.

They did look a bit unusual. Being honest, they mostly looked like zombies. The woman at the front had a chalk-white face, a bone-white dress, and thick tresses of lustrous black hair tumbling down her back. I'm not sure all that hair was entirely hers. I'm also not sure that the red stuff dribbling from one corner of her mouth was her real blood either. It did look convincing though.

She was with a man in a top hat and tailcoat. But the coat looked like it had been slashed with a knife and the top hat looked like it had been hit with a hammer. They were arguing about a ring. As they argued, they jabbed their fingers at each other. A really loud bell bonged once, then twice, slowly. When we looked up there was a man – dressed all in black – saying, 'Please will the bride-and-groom-to-be enter the Gloom.'

That's when we found out it was a wedding.

Brodie said, 'People come to Las Vegas to get married

178

in a hurry. It's called 'Sign and Go'. They just go in, sign a piece of paper, then they're married and off they go. This is someone's happy day. We should leave.'

Obviously, Nathan had different ideas.

Nathan followed the bride and groom through the tombstone doorway with his head bowed down like a pageboy. I tried my best to look like a bridesmaid.

Brodie said, 'I'm not sure about this.' But he followed us in anyway.

The inside of the Till Death Doth Us Part wedding chapel did NOT look wedding-y. In the glow of a thousand tiny bone-shaped fairy lights, little glass skeleton ornaments twinkled, dancing in and out of spiky cactuses.

We were slightly conspicuous, to be honest. Especially as we were children, not zombies. But that didn't matter because the bride and groom only had eyes for each other. Screwed up, angry eyes. They were still jabbing fingers at each other and arguing. It seemed the groom had lost the ring.

A door opened and a man in a long black cape swept into the room in a cloud of smoke. 'My dear, dear children of the night,' he boomed, 'you have come here to vow your unDYING love before the law and me – Count Love. Allow me to WARN you that you have only paid for the ten-minute service. If your argument continues, you may have to pay another one hundred dollars. Bring forth your witnesses.'

'Witnesses?' snarled the bride. 'He hasn't even brought the ring.'

'I did bring the ring,' said the groom. 'I've just dropped it somewhere. That's all.'

Count Love pointed at us and beckoned, saying, 'Witnesses, advance.'

'They're not our witnesses,' snapped the bride. 'They're nothing to do with us. If you think we're paying extra to have . . . Is that a rabbit? That can't be a rabbit.'

'She is a rabbit. She's just a bit large. She came second in the Massive Rabbits class at the Lancashire show.'

'I didn't ask for a rabbit at my wedding.' The bride looked us up and down as if she'd never seen children before. 'What even are you?' she said. 'Hobbits, or what?'

Nathan took this as cue to start a show.

'Good question,' he said. 'What do you think of –' he strolled up to the bride, with a Hobbity roll to his stroll '– when you think of Hobbits?'

Count Love and the groom started to list off all kinds of Hobbit features – hairy feet, smoking pipes, and so on.

The bride snapped, 'If you keep talking, we're going to have to pay another one hundred dollars. Just shut up and let's get married. Forget the rings.'

'Rings!' said Nathan. 'Exactly. When it comes to

rings, you can always trust a Hobbit. So. Give me your hands . . .'

They didn't know Nathan from a bat in a barn, but they still did what he asked. That's part of a magician's skill set – getting people to do what you ask. He joined their hands, closed his eyes, and said, 'Now look at your hands.'

The bride looked at her hand, amazed. The missing wedding ring was on her finger. 'How . . . ?' she gasped. 'How did you do that? Are you actually magic?! Look! He's actually magic.'

To quote Karabas the Modest, *'Ninety per cent of magic is noticing the things that other people don't notice.'* The groom didn't notice he'd dropped the ring in the street earlier, but Nathan did. He took a bow and said, 'Give me a ring sometime. Ha ha!'

The groom looked grumpy and suspicious. 'Does this mean we're married now?' he said.

'Of course it means we're married!' said the bride. 'Married by an actual magic person. What did you think it meant?! Don't you WANT to be married?'

The moment she said that, all the lights went out. The floor began to shake.

And it felt like the end of the world.

CHAPTER THIRTY-ONE

HALF A WORLD AWAY

BRODIE:

Animals can predict earthquakes and tsunamis. Everyone says so. All the mice and lizards left Pompeii days before the volcano blew up. If people had just paid attention to the mice and lizards, they would have been OK.

I paid attention to Queenie when she jumped out of my arms and ran out of the wedding while the bride and groom were still arguing about being married. So I was already outside when the ground began to move.

MIDDY:

Count Love said it wasn't an earthquake, just a light second-wave tremor. 'Earth tremors are best enjoyed outdoors,' he said. 'Please leave by the tomb exit.'

The fairy lights swayed from the ceiling. The little glass skeletons rang like tiny bells as they shivered on their shelves. A biro rolled out from under one of the chairs and then rolled back under again. I caught a cactus as it bounced off a shelf.

Nathan grabbed my arm and we ran. Then we were outside. No one in the queue seemed that fussed about the possibility of the ground opening up and swallowing everyone. The ground shakes so often in Las Vegas that they have What to Do in an Earthquake lessons in school. So everyone just stood around chatting.

Then the lights went out.

The lights in Fremont, Las Vegas are not like Blackpool Illuminations. They're not pretty little twinkly sea creatures. They're nearly all words. Words that flash on and off; words that flicker and flare; words that spin round.

HOT DOGS! COLD DRINKS! S T A R T I N G NOW! COMING SOON! ENTER!

ENTERTAINMENT! EXIT! EXCITEMENT! COME IN! KEEP OUT!

It's like being shouted at by light.

So when they all – *pop* – went out, it wasn't the dark that hit us. It was the quiet.

It was so quiet.

The ground had stopped wobbling. The tremor was over. But the lights had not come back on.

So there I was standing, lost, in the dark, in a city on the wrong side of the world, with no tricks to show, and no chance of getting to see Perplexion.

I was thinking we should have just let the police catch us back at the hotel. The worst that could happen was not as bad as this. I was wishing the ground really would open and swallow me up. I was wishing I never listened to a word our Nathan said about anything, especially his dream.

That's when Nathan nudged me and said, 'Do they have a different moon in America, or what?'

And I looked up at the sky.

And – oh.

Just like at home in Blackpool, when the lights for miles around were switched off, the sky was switched on. There was one big difference here though. At home, by the sea, we'd seen thick clouds of stars. But here, tonight, the most amazing thing was the moon. It really did look like a different moon. Not light and silvery like back home. This was a big, fat, juicy-looking moon. It looked heavy, like it might fall out of the sky and splat like a ripe orange. Because it was orange. Not silver or white like at home.

I said, 'No, Nathan, it's the same old moon. It just looks more wonderful than usual, that's all.'

'It's pollution from the cars that make it look a different colour,' said Brodie.

'Maybe,' I said, 'but I think you're missing the point.'

I was thinking about the moon and the stars and how they're always there and always amazing as long as you remember to look up.

I was thinking about something Karabas had said . . .

Everything – even the most ordinary everyday object – has magic in it. A playing card, a shell, a pea, a pencil, a paper clip, a pen – they are all full of magic. Your job is to wake that magic up!

To make it shine out. To remind the audience that they live among wonders.

Karabas the Modest, *My Secrets Revealed*

I looked down at my hands. I didn't have a pack of cards, or a set of shells and peas. But I was holding that cactus. The cactus that had just dropped into my hands as if by magic.

Ta-dah.

CHAPTER THIRTY-TWO

CONJURING BY CANDLELIGHT

NATHAN:

I knew what Middy was thinking. I always know what she's thinking. When she looked up at the moon and down at the cactus, I knew a trick was coming.

I followed her down the street, and so did Brodie and Queenie. The lights were still off.

A few minutes before, we'd thought we were going to see the whole city fall into a hole in the ground. Now it was just dark and hushed. But we still had the feeling that something was going to happen.

We followed Middy round the corner.

Up ahead, warm yellow light was pouring out of an open doorway onto the street.

'How have they got light?' said Brodie. 'There's no electricity.'

As we got closer to the building, we saw that it was candles, hundreds of them, all blazing away in the nooks and crannies on candlesticks, casting their glow onto statues of men and women.

'It's a church,' said Brodie.

'Bienvenidos a Santa Brígida,' said a tiny woman in a headscarf as we peeped in. 'Bienvenidos a todos. Come in. Come in. When the electricity goes, we open the doors. Like a very small lighthouse. See?'

But as soon as we were properly in the light, she stepped back. 'Oh,' she said, 'Madre de Dios. You're just children.'

Brodie pointed out that we were not just children. We were children plus a rabbit.

'Little children,' said the headscarf woman, 'and a big rabbit. But where are your parents?'

We didn't bother mentioning that they were on the other side of the world. We just smiled. She flapped around us.

'We have some biscuits,' she said, opening a tin. And then she went, 'Oh, look! From the fiesta.' She gave us Oreos, some squeaky tinselly things, and a fistful of party poppers and balloons. She seemed to think we were hungry toddlers and it was our birthday.

Anyway, she must've thought that biscuits and balloons were all the help we'd ever need, because she went back to a little crowd of people around the door and they said a prayer together. Even though it was in a language I couldn't understand, I could tell it was the 'Our Father'.

I said to Middy, 'The prayers are the same as the ones at home. Even if the moon is different.'

Middy said, 'I told you, the moon is not different here. And of course the prayers are the same. Jesus didn't only come to Blackpool, you know.'

The little crowd of people went back to chatting, probably about when the electricity was going to come back on. Every now and then one of them would look out into the street, as if they thought the electricity might come and knock at the door. I was thinking, *These people have nothing to do; maybe we could entertain them.*

So I gave them a bit of magic.

There was a woman cradling a little girl in her arms, just next to the statue of Saint Brígida. I offered the little girl an Oreo. She took it and then I mimed that she should eat it. But when she looked in her hand – no Oreo. Her little face drooped with disappointment. I didn't want her to start crying, so I offered her another Oreo right away. She took it with her right hand. I pointed to her left hand. She opened her hand and there was another Oreo. Her face completely glowed with surprise at the unexpected extra biscuit. She said some things in Spanish. I didn't understand the words, but it didn't matter. Magic speaks wonder. Everyone was laughing and chatting. A minute before, they had been just a bunch of people waiting for the electricity to come back on. Now they were a kind of party.

Then Middy decided to do her trick.

It was probably not a good decision.

CHAPTER THIRTY-THREE

MILLION DOLLAR MIRACLE

MIDDY:

Magic doesn't come when you're trying, but it does come by trying. If you keep thinking and practising, the magic idea will come when you're not looking. The magician's brain likes to do its own special misdirection.

Karabas the Modest, *My Secrets Revealed*

Honestly, when I got the idea for how to make my trick work, it seemed like magic. I was looking up at the statue in the back of the church. It was a woman holding a box that looked just like my lunchbox trick. Apparently she's Saint Brígida.

Anyway, I was standing there, wishing an ingenious idea would materialize, when the woman in the headscarf put those balloons and party poppers in my hand with a big smile.

'Regalo. Present.' And she winked at me.

I looked at the balloons and at the cactus, and that was it. I knew exactly how to make it work. The idea came to me like a present. And just like a present it needed a cardboard box. Luckily there was one there in the corner with a few candles left in it.

Everyone seemed to be enjoying Nathan's party tricks so much, I decided to step things up a little. So I did my extra-special trick without even practising or telling them what I was going to do.

You should never ever do that.

I should have remembered what Karabas the Modest said in the very first chapter of *My Secrets Revealed*:

> *There's a time and a place for magic. If you're sitting in a theatre and I open a box to reveal a fierce tiger, you might say, 'Good heavens, a fierce tiger!'*
>
> *If, on the other hand, you are sitting on a train and I open a box to release a fierce tiger, you would be more likely to shout for help.*
>
> *Always, always read the room.*

Maybe I hadn't remembered that bit of *My Secrets Revealed* but I soon found out how true it was.

As soon as I did the trick there was chaos. I probably

looked a bit spooky – a girl standing there in the candlelight – and then I made this impossible thing happen. The headscarf lady dropped to her knees shouting, 'Madre de Dios, ayúdanos!' and started crossing herself over and over. A couple of people ran away into the night.

CAPTAIN JIMENEZ:

At this point, the boy, Nathan, tried to get the girl, Middy, to show me her trick. I said that wouldn't be necessary. He said, 'Maybe later.' I said, 'Maybe.'

He said, 'When we perform that trick on-stage, here in Las Vegas in front of some of the greatest magicians in the world, you'll see it then.'

I said, 'I highly doubt that.'

MIDDY:

Then a small nun barged into the group shouting, 'Why are you scaring Señora Torres! Her heart is very bad. She could be dead any minute. What did you do? I will call the police.'

She pulled a mobile out of her sleeve and held it up to her furious little face, which was peeping out from under this big, flappy veil.

I wasn't sure how to answer, so I did the trick again. I know I know, you're not supposed to do the same trick twice. But I actually did it a lot better the second time.

Everything changed.

The nun's face came out from under the veil. It wasn't furious any more. She clapped her hands and said, 'Estupendo, estupendo.'

I didn't know what the word meant, but we understood the smile. It was the same big happy-baby smile you see whenever a trick goes right. It was the smile that Miss Khoshroo had given Nathan that day in the playground years ago.

The people who were hiding behind the font realized I was just a little English girl.

The nun said, 'Venid. Venid conmigo. Come.'

And we followed her back through the church, along a dark corridor and into the kitchen. There were four or five nuns sitting around the table playing cards and eating Pop Tarts.. The biggest one was reading to the others by candlelight from some kind of nun book. I think she was Boss Nun. When we came in she looked up and spoke in English.

'Well what have we here, Sister Boniface?'

'A miracle,' said our little nun. Then she asked

me to show the others.

I said it wasn't a miracle, just a trick.

Boss Nun said, 'You can leave the theology to us.'

So I did it again. Honestly, it got better every time. It went really well.

All the nuns gasped, then laughed, then clapped.

Except Boss Nun. She sat there with that nun book in her fist, frowning so deep her veil was nearly touching her eyebrows. 'There's something,' she said, 'missing.'

'Like what, Sister?'

Our little nun said Boss Nun wasn't 'Sister'. 'This is Mother,' she said. 'Mother Amelia.'

'It's just a trick,' said Mother Amelia. 'It doesn't, you know, SAY anything. When David Copperfield made the Statue of Liberty vanish, it made you think about what the world would be like without Liberty. Or when David Blaine turned a homeless man's cup of coffee into a cup of money, that was emotional because the man needed money.'

The other nuns all agreed that that was a really emotional trick.

'I was in floods of tears at that one,' said Sister Boniface.

All the nuns seemed to know a lot about magic. But then I suppose they were Las Vegas nuns.

'When my own saint – Boniface – gave poor

children stones and turned them into candy,' said Sister Boniface, 'he was saying, *You children deserve the good things in life*. What is your trick SAYING?'

'It's saying, *Look at me. I'm clever*,' said Mother Amelia. 'That's all.'

'I didn't know a trick had to say anything. I thought being magic was enough.'

'Magic,' said Mother Amelia, 'is one thing. What you really need is wonder. We make our lives predictable. We forget that life is wonderful – that it's wonderful that people thought of creating books or phones or food, or building a city in the desert. We forget. The job of magic is to remind us. For instance, why do people come and spend their money in Las Vegas? Because all their lives when they spend one dollar in a shop, they get one dollar's worth of shopping back. In Las Vegas they are hoping that one dollar will give them a million dollars back. They spend dollar after dollar hoping that one of those dollars will give them a million dollars.'

'Or thirty-nine million,' said Brodie.

By now I was really wanting to quiz Mother Amelia about where she had learned so much about magic, but then the lights came on. The electricity was back!

The nuns cheered. And clapped. The fridge-freezer buzzed into life. The washing machine in the corner started up again.

'You see,' said Mother Amelia, 'now we all remember that electricity is wonderful.'

There was a TV on the wall above the store cupboards. That flickered on too. When a TV comes on, you look at it. So everyone looked at the screen. But then, straight away, everyone turned round to look at Brodie. Because Brodie was on the TV. Just a photo of him, looking a bit intense.

The newsreader with eyebrows that went up and down like a fairground ride said:

'Staff at the Camelot Casino Hotel are searching for this lucky young man. Earlier today his single-dollar stake won him four point five million dollars on the famous 'GOLDEN

OLDIE' *Mega Bucks machine, before he mysteriously ran away without his prize. This is the second time this machine has paid out big. Got to say, if I was the hotel manager, I would unplug it, but . . .'*

No one was listening.

Everyone was staring at Brodie.

'Four,' said Mother Amelia, 'point five,' she went on, 'million –' she was finding it hard to keep talking – 'dollars?'

'And,' said Sister Boniface, 'you ran away?'

'We've talked a lot about wonder,' said Mother Amelia. 'But what I'm wondering now is, what's going on here?'

CHAPTER THIRTY-FOUR

TRUST. THE. DREAM.

BRODIE:

Mother Amelia switched off the TV and told us to
help ourselves to Pop Tarts. Sister Boniface blew out
all the candles and chivvied everyone back into the
street. Out there, the lights were punching the air and
shouting their slogans again.

Nathan told the nuns all about his dream of doing
magic in Las Vegas with Middy. Middy told them all
about our mission to bring back the Tower.

But all I could think was . . . *What just happened?*

Even the nuns weren't really listening. Sister
Boniface handed Middy her mobile and told her to
call her parents. But Middy didn't know their phone
number. I mean who knows anyone's phone number?

Mother Amelia said not to worry. She'd already
phoned the police. She said Las Vegas was a dangerous
place at the best of times. 'And now one of you has
hit the jackpot, you'll be targets for any kind of gnarly

villain you care to name – fraudsters, confidence tricksters, kidnappers . . .'

There were lots of others. She seemed to know a lot of different types of villain.

'But Nathan's dream . . .' said Middy.

'Dreams are just dreams,' said Mother Amelia. 'If dreams came true, I would find myself flying up the stairs instead of climbing them.'

'Oh!' said Sister Boniface, 'I have flying-up-the-stairs dreams too.'

Then they began googling the time difference between Las Vegas and Blackpool and having a conversation about whether it would be all right to contact the Blackpool police in the middle of the night.

That was the first time I'd heard anyone mention the time difference. It seemed strange to think that Mum and Dad and everyone at home were already in tomorrow, and we were in yesterday.

'But this is our last chance to see Perplexion,' wailed Middy.

'So sad,' said Sister Boniface, 'that he's leaving show business. All the great magicians will be there.'

'Those tickets are a fierce price,' said Mother Amelia.

Then everyone stopped talking. Everyone looked at me. Everyone was thinking the same thought. But I was the one who said it out loud.

'We have four point five million dollars. So we can afford it.'

'Exactly,' said Nathan. 'We were on the other side of the world. And now here we are, in the right place. We had no way of getting tickets. And now we have. You have to admit, some kind of magic is happening here. TRUST. THE. DREAM. PEOPLE.' And being honest, I WAS beginning to trust the dream.

'Hmmm,' said Mother Amelia, raising one eyebrow.

Down the corridor a bell was ringing.

'Time,' she said, 'for evening prayer. Then we'll find some phone chargers so you can look up your parents' phone numbers. Help yourselves to the Pop Tarts.'

All the nuns filed out. Nathan got up and took a big, colourful box from the shelf.

I said to him, 'What are you doing?'

He said, 'I'm helping myself to Pop Tarts, like she said. I've always wanted to try Pop Tarts.'

I said, 'Give your head a shake, Nathan. We can't hang around eating Pop Tarts. The police are going to be here any second. And I've got millions of pounds to collect.'

'Yeah but we can't just stroll back into the hotel. Like Mother Amelia said, your face has been on TV. Everyone knows you're rich. You could be robbed or taken hostage or anything.'

'We've got to get back in there somehow,' said Middy. 'The show starts soon. But how? We can't just stroll back in.'

I said, 'I'm the oldest. I'm in charge. I say we ARE going the Camelot. Because I have a plan.'

CHAPTER THIRTY-FIVE

NO ONE MESSES WITH A NUN

NATHAN:

Going back to the Camelot Casino Hotel disguised as nuns was a cracking notion.

The safest I've felt in my life was walking along the Strip in Las Vegas that evening dressed as a nun.

We did leave the nuns a thank-you note, for looking after us, also for the Pop Tarts. Then we slipped on the nun clothes and slipped out of the back door.

CAPTAIN JIMENEZ:

The girl, Middy, apologised for adding to
Las Vegas' crime statistics. 'I'm sure you
do your best Captain Jimenez,' she said. 'We realise
that stealing nun clothes is also a crime, so we were
actually adding to the crime statistics while we were
trying to keep ourselves safe. Sorry about that.'

MIDDY:

It's true. The nun disguises really worked.
 No one beats up nuns. No one tries to steal
stuff from nuns. Or kidnaps nuns.
 No one even tries to stop nuns.

We breezed into the Camelot Casino Hotel. People said, 'Good evening, Sisters,' in a right friendly way. As we hurried through the casino keeping our hoods pulled down over our faces, we looked like Jedi nuns. Someone even asked us to say a prayer for them before they threw their dice.

'I just need a five,' he said.

I said, 'Dear God, let this man throw a five with these dice, Amen.'

But Nathan obviously had to nun things up a bit.

'My dear child,' he said – to the old guy. 'My dear child, let us pray that the Lord makes your dice land on number five and that you win loads of money and use that money to do good in the world . . .'

'Amen,' said the old man, but Nathan wasn't finished.

'That your servant . . . What's your name? God needs to know your name?'

'Dwayne.'

'That your servant Dwayne's dice come up three and two or four and one, doesn't matter which, and that he then goes forth to help the poor people with his winnings so that—'

'I don't want to do that. I just want money. For a motorbike.'

'Well, OK,' said Nathan. 'Amen then.'

I said, 'Can we get moving now, Sister?'

It seemed mad to me that these people were just getting on with their cards and dice and slot machines while the very last chance to see the greatest living magician was about to start just a few yards away.

The man rolled the dice. He threw two twos, so he lost his money. Then he stepped in front of Brodie, and I thought, *This is it. The End. They know who we are.* But he said, 'That didn't work. Can I tickle this here rabbit's paw for luck, Sister?'

He stroked Queenie's furry paw. Threw his dice again and won most of his money back.

We got out of the casino bit, and through an archway with stone lions, and then there it was . . . the portcullis that lets you into the theatre. And on the big screen above the portcullis a sign flashed:

Perplexion . . . The Master's Final Mystery . . . POSTPONED.
DUE TO EARTH TREMOR

Postponed. No. Postponed? After all this. Then the sign flashed again . . .

Until the Magic Hour - MIDNIGHT.

I stared at Nathan. He shrugged. 'Trust the dream,' he said.

CHAPTER THIRTY-SIX

POP TARTS!

MIDDY:

As soon as I knew we still had time to see Perplexion before his show, my brain started to fizz. Everything I looked at seemed to give me an idea about how to make my new trick better. And by the way, nun clothes. Nun clothes are ideal for magic. They've got big sleeves. Long skirts. Proper pockets. A veil. I said to Nathan, 'We should do our act dressed up as nuns. We could call ourselves the Wonder Sisters.'

'I can't be a Sister,' he said, 'I'm a boy.'

'Well, I'm a girl, but I'm a Wonder Brother.'

'Can we please,' said Brodie, 'go to reception now and claim my four point five million dollars.'

Reception was crowded like the Blackpool Prom on the Big Switch-On night. People were pushing and shoving and shouting all around the desk.

Brodie said maybe a coach party had just arrived and they were all trying to book in. But it wasn't that. There was something strange about the crowd. Something not very Las Vegas.

'Kids,' said Nathan. 'We've barely seen any children since we got here, and now there's all these kids.'

'Boys,' I said. 'They're all boys.'

This wasn't a queue of people waiting to check in. This was a queue of mums and dads, each one of them trying to claim that their child was the one who'd put the lucky dollar in the slot, won four and a half million dollars and run away.

'What,' said Nathan, 'a crowd of liars. At least we don't have to queue with them.'

'How come?'

'Trust me.'

It was true. Nathan strolled right up to the desk, and people stood back to let us past. He kept saying, 'Bless you' to them and sometimes, quietly, 'God forgive you.'

Behind the desk there was another woman in a Maid Marian outfit. Only this one looked more like a Maid Marian who'd had a fight with Friar Tuck in a ditch with a quarterstaff in a high wind.

'Prithee!' she bawled. 'All calm thyselves right down, else I will have thee all ejected. By Sir Galahad. With a lance. You won't like it.'

People stepped back a bit. None of their kids looked even a bit like Brodie, by the way.

Maid Marian looked at us and snarled, 'There's a queue, Sisters.'

'But, child,' said Nathan in his nun voice. He really seemed to love being a nun. 'Know ye not who we are?'

Maid Marian looked puzzled. 'Are you,' she whispered, 'staff? Are you the nuns who look after King Arthur when he's wounded or something? Because if you are, I could use some help here. Real quick. There's going to be a brawl.'

'We,' said Nathan, his voice muffled by his veil, 'know the whereabouts of the boy who won the money.'

Maid Marian rolled her eyes. 'There's a hundred angry adults with a hundred kids ahead of you in the queue. Get to the back.'

'We know something they don't,' said Nathan. 'This wasn't mentioned or shown on the TV . . .'

'Go on.'

'The boy. He was carrying a large rabbit, was he not?'

At last, Maid Marian looked interested.

'Could it be,' said Nathan, 'this rabbit?'

He nodded at Brodie. Brodie lifted Queenie up for her to see.

'Wait,' said Maid Marian. She bawled at the crowd again, 'All ye who are pushing,' she shouted, 'shall be defenestrated. If ye don't know what it means, sir, I'll happily demonstrate. You won't like it.'

210

Then she said quietly. 'See the Staff Only door over there? Go and wait in there. Help yourself to drinks and nibbles. Someone will come to confirm your identity and give you the money. Don't run now. Don't make a fuss. This crowd is in an ugly mood.'

So we strolled over to the Staff Only door. There was a couch, a toaster, a mini fridge and . . .

'Pop Tarts!' said Nathan. 'We get to try them after all.'

'I'll take off my nun disguise,' said Brodie, 'so they can see it's me.'

'No, no,' said Nathan. 'Be careful. Let's take no chances. We'll just say we've got the boy safe somewhere. Until we're sure we can trust them.'

Pop Tarts, by the way. What a disappointment. They're basically ready-made jam butties, which you put in the toaster. The jam comes out lava-hot and blisters your tongue. Then – in case the jam isn't sweet enough – there's sugar on the outside too. It was all we could do to finish the packet before the door opened and someone came in.

The person who came in had little round dark glasses, red hair and a steak bake in each hand. It was Perplexion's bodyguard. Nathan stood up, and brushed the bits of Pop Tart from his skirt.

'Excuse me,' he said with a smile. 'Crumbs all over my nun clothes.'

'Habit,' said Mr Steak Bake.

'Oh no,' said Nathan. 'It's the first Pop Tart I've ever eaten. You're looking for the boy who—'

'They're called habits,' said Mr Steak Bake, in his voice like chip shop gravy, 'not nun clothes. As for the kid, I was with him when he had his stroke of luck . . .'

'How fortunate.'

'So I'll know him when I see him,' said Mr Steak Bake.

'Indeed,' said Nathan. 'We have him safe in our nun house—'

'Convent,' said the man, placing his hand on Brodie's head. Then, like a magician pulling a line of

flags from his sleeve, he plucked the veil from Brodie's head.

Busted.

'We knew you'd come if you heard about the money,' he said. 'You haven't won anything, by the way. You were too young to be inside a casino, let alone playing the machines. So your winnings don't count. And as an employee of Perplexion and Co. Mysteries Incorporated, I'm not allowed to play either. The machine was just teasing the both of us.'

'That is disappointing,' said Nathan. 'Well, we must be going. It's almost nun bedtime.'

'You're going all right.' Mr Steak Bake smiled. 'Hear those sirens? That's the police. You're going with them.'

Unfortunately for him he sat on Queenie's Stars and Stripes hat and slipped off the chair. He tried to grab Nathan but all he got was a handful of nun's habit.

I suppose three half-dressed nuns running across reception is always going to attract attention. Especially if there's a fleet of police cars pulling up outside.

That's when Nathan decided to walk up to the patrol car and demand that the officer arrest Perplexion.

And that's how we ended up here.

So that's everything that's happened to us so far.

What happens next is up to you, Captain Jimenez.

CHAPTER THIRTY-SEVEN

FOR THE RECORD . . .

CAPTAIN JIMENEZ:

I've spent today trying to swallow an extra–large portion of these kids' stories.

For the record, here's what they've told me:

1. They're a magic act from England, going by the name the Wonder Brothers.
2. They're from a town called Blackpool, which has inexplicably lost its famous landmark Tower. Which they then inexplicably promised to find.
3. They have come to Las Vegas 'by accident'.
4. They are accusing Perplexion – Master of Mystery – of stealing the famous landmark Tower.

By the way, there is zero evidence of Perplexion wandering about the place with a five-hundred-foot landmark sticking out of his back pocket.

When the boy Nathan, suggested searching

Perplexion's room, I said, 'If we went to the Camelot Casino Hotel right now and searched his room, my guess is we would not find that five-hundred-foot metal Tower hidden under his bed.'

Furthermore:

5. The boy, Nathan, had some kind of dream that they would do their act on-stage here in Vegas. The girl believes she can persuade the Master of Mystery to return their famous landmark by showing him a magic trick.
6. They have a rabbit with them.

Also for the record: A summary of how much I believe of their story:

Not much.

I told them that children should not be allowed to wander the streets of Las Vegas. Period. Especially if the streets of Las Vegas are five thousand miles away from where you belong. It's time to get off the dream bus and onto the plane home.

'And now,' I said, 'I'll leave you in the capable hands of Sergeant Jamie. It's time for me to leave. You see, I have an urgent appointment.'

The flights are booked. They have tickets for the first UK-bound plane out of Vegas. They will fly as unaccompanied minors. Sergeant Jamie will drive them to the airport. That brings Operation Tower to a satisfactory conclusion.

SIGNED: CAPTAIN JIMENEZ

CHAPTER THIRTY-EIGHT

DON'T YOU WANT TO KNOW WHAT HAPPENS NEXT?

SERGEANT JAMIE:

I have been asked by my superior officer to give my version of events. Here's what happened next. As far as I remember. To be honest, it's all somewhat of a blur.

We were in my patrol car heading westbound.

I did say to the kids, 'Your dream was just a dream. That's a hard lesson to learn, but you're in the right place to learn it. You know what they say, *Las Vegas is where dreams come to die.*'

I remember we were approaching the luxury Camelot Casino Hotel, when I put on Radio Green Field. The atmosphere was tense. I tried my best to jolly things up, mentioning that 'Green Fields' is what 'Las Vegas' means in English. Sort of. You wouldn't think it to look around Las Vegas now. I find little nuggets of information can cheer a soul up when they're down. Or under arrest.

I seem to remember the tune they were playing was 'Magic Bullet', but, whatever – as soon as it finished, there was an announcement. DJ Chip Friday said live on air:

'The mystery British kid deemed too young to win the Mega Bucks jackpot might still have Lady Luck on his side. The good people of this city that never sleeps filled our message boards with love and fury. And . . . the luxury Camelot Casino Hotel listened! They have made the magical offer of TWO free tickets to see the world-exclusive one-night-only show that everyone is talking about – and, yes, I do mean Perplexion, Master of Mystery's final show. That's what we in Las Vegas call . . . a dream come true.'

'Did you hear that?' said the boy Nathan.

'I heard it,' I said.

'Our dream is literally about to come true. Don't you want to know what happens? Are you going to drive past actual magic?'

I considered this for a moment. I checked my watch. Could they catch the show and still catch the plane? It looked like they could. So I said, 'No, sir, I am not.'

At that point, instead of continuing on the Strip in

the direction of Harry Reid International Airport, as instructed by my commanding officer, I defied orders and took the exit for the Camelot Casino Hotel.

I mean, come on. This has to be real magic.

As I turned into the hotel, the girl said, *'Ta-dah.'* The boy, Nathan, said, 'Wonders.' And the other one said, 'Two tickets? But there's three of us, and I'm the one who won the jackpot.'

CHAPTER THIRTY-NINE

SIT BACK AND ENJOY THE SHOW

MIDDY:

They say the biggest, scariest thing any magician can do is try to fool another magician. That night, Perplexion wasn't planning to fool one other magician. He was planning to fool ALL the other magicians. At least all the famous ones who are still alive. They were all there, in the front few rows. As we walked into the theatre we saw:

David Copperfield (made the Statue of Liberty vanish)
Criss Angel (levitated off the top of the Luxor Hotel)
Fay Presto (can push a bottle straight through a
    wooden table)
Chris Ramsay (master of cardistry)
Chris Pilsworth (the magic of laughter)
David Blaine (turned coffee into money)
Dynamo (walks on water)
Dorothy Dietrich (bullet–catcher)

There was so much magic in the room, you felt that the whole place might float off into the air any minute. If Blackpool is the home of magic, Las Vegas is its holiday home.

Nathan was, like, 'Middy, this is it. This is exactly like in my dream. We are going to do this!'

I said, 'No. We definitely are not. There is no way we are going to attempt to do magic in front of this crowd.'

'You'll see,' he said.

The lights went down.

Some music played.

A tiny spotlight appeared in the middle of the stage. Very slowly. Like a flower, it began to grow.

I said, 'He's building up the sense of anticipation.'

'Maybe,' said Nathan, 'we should just go down there right now and do it.'

'We won't be doing any magic,' I said. 'Just enjoy the show.'

Because suddenly the music stopped and all the lights went off on-stage. As if the show was over.

An announcer said the theatre was sorry, but there had been a technical problem. Someone came onto the stage in a hard yellow hat, checked shirt and overalls. They dropped their tool box on the floor and started checking all the footlights and the microphones. Nathan nudged me and said they must be an electrician, like my dad. The announcer kept saying they were sorry for the delay. Everyone started to get a bit restless.

Then the electrician goes and drags a chair onto the stage, roots around in their tool box, takes out a lunchbox and sits down.

'That lunchbox . . .' I whispered.

'I know,' said Nathan. 'It's just like the one you made. The exploding one. I can't believe Perplexion has stolen your trick.'

'Well,' I said. 'The trick is hundreds of years old. I just made it better.'

The electrician plonked the lunchbox down on the stage, stretched, and lifted the lid . . .

BANG!

The box expanded. Just like mine! But also not like mine. Mine expanded to something just about big enough to house a large rabbit. This looked more like a wardrobe. It had a door in the front.

Perplexion had made it bigger. Like a hundred times bigger.

Everyone cheered and clapped. The show had started.

The electrician made a deep bow and straightened up. During the bow, the hard hat fell off and clattered onto the stage. During the straightening up, the check shirt and overalls seemed to glitch. And there, was Zenith, in the fiery red dress. Like magic.

She opened the door in the front of the expanded wardrobe and . . . everyone held their breath . . . waiting for the Master of Mystery himself to step out of there, onto the stage . . .

Except he didn't.

Someone did step out. But it wasn't Perplexion.

The magicians were cheering because they knew that this trick had been around for two hundred years, but no one had really been able to make it work – until now.

The person stepped out, just looking a bit confused, and stood blinking in the spotlight, shielding his eyes. He said, 'Hello? Oh. Have I come out on the stage? The person was . . . Brodie.

I whispered to Nathan, 'Was this in your dream? Brodie was on stage and not us?!'

Brodie was squinting into the spotlight. 'Sorry,' he said. 'Not sure. The other two had tickets so . . .'

We couldn't hear what else he said because everyone was laughing. They thought it was part of the show.

Zenith looked confused. But not as confused as Brodie.

'Stage fright,' said Nathan. 'Brodie doesn't know what to do. He's like a rabbit stuck in the headlights.'

Right on cue, Queenie – the most stage-struck rabbit in history – bounced out of the wardrobe into the spotlight, sat up on her haunches, wiggled her ears and did a little bow. The audience proper loved her. But I knew we couldn't leave Brodie there just dithering about the stage.

I whispered to Nathan, 'He's stuck. We've got to help him.'

Nathan didn't answer. He just sat there staring straight ahead.

'Come on. We've got to get down there and save him.'

'Can't.'

'What?'

'Can't.'

'Come on. Trust the dream.'

'Can't.'

All around us the applause was dying down. People were shuffling forward in their seats waiting to see what would happen next. But we knew nothing was going to happen. Queenie's smart, but she is just a very big rabbit.

'Nathan,' I hissed. 'This is it. This is exactly what you dreamed.'

'I didn't dream,' he said.

'WHAT?' I nearly shouted.

Nathan shrugged. 'There was no dream. Well not exactly. I just said that to keep your spirits up. It was just a story.'

I felt so confused. 'But everything you said came true.'

'I mostly said things after they happened,' admitted Nathan.

'So . . .' I looked him in the eye.

'Can't,' he said.

'Well,' I said, 'I can.'

Oh. Wait. I haven't told you what the trick is yet. You'll need to know otherwise this won't make sense. Being honest, it's a good one.

I blow up the balloon and . . . well, it's an illusion where I use a balloon, a cactus and a cardboard box. The finale of the trick – what we magicians call the prestige – is me holding up a cactus INSIDE a balloon. A beautiful, impossible thing. Beautiful and impossible enough for anyone, you'd think.

I grabbed the balloons and cactus from my magic backpack and climbed up onto the stage. I didn't have a cardboard box so I borrowed Zenith's tool box.

I blew up the balloon, and bounced it on the cactus. I let it burst. I did that just to spin things out a bit.

It was a good move.

When a balloon bursts, a person jumps. Brodie and Queenie really jumped. I told them to sit down and get their breath back. That got a laugh, and the balloon burst got everyone's attention. It also proved that the cactus needles really were sharp and reminded people – in case they'd forgotten – that balloons burst easily.

When I was blowing up the second balloon, I could see all the most famous living magicians on earth leaning forward, wondering what was going to happen. That's the genius of getting it wrong to start with. It makes getting it right in the end more exciting. They were on my side. They were willing it to work for me.

Behind them I could see Mother Amelia and Sister Boniface beaming away at me. And the faces of some of the people I'd seen shovelling money into the slot machines in the casino earlier. I bounced another balloon onto the spikes. When that second balloon burst, I said, 'Unlucky.'

It was all I needed to say. Everyone in Las Vegas knows what unlucky means. Everyone in Las Vegas knows that unlucky is normal and that lucky is magic.

Oh page thirty eight of *My Secrets Revealed*, Karabas the Modest says, '*Magicians always say the hand is quicker than the eye. Of course it isn't! The eye sees at the speed of light. Three hundred million metres per second. Nothing in the whole universe is quicker than that. Only one thing is faster than the speed of light. A good story. With the right story you can make every eye in the room look in the wrong place. Then it doesn't matter how slow your hand moves.'*

As soon as I said 'unlucky' people's brains told them they were watching a story about someone who kept losing but carried on hoping and trying.

One more balloon . . .

I said, 'Third time lucky?'

The tension in that theatre was like . . . well, it was like a balloon blown up right to its limit.

So far I'd messed it up on purpose. But if I messed up for real, that would be like letting go of a blown-up balloon. All I'd get would be one long rude noise.

As though I'd given up, I dropped the cactus into the tool box. Then I shoved the balloon in after it. Really hard. Everyone caught their breath. Surely there would be a bang this time.

I put my hand into the tool box and pulled the balloon out again. But something was different. Now the cactus was inside the balloon. I lifted the balloon over my head, into the spotlight so everyone could see. A balloon with a spiky cactus inside. A beautiful, impossible thing.

A balloon with a spiky cactus inside. Beautiful, impossible, magic.

The audience loved it. They clapped. They cheered.

When I say 'they', by the way, yes, I do mean *everyone*. EVEN Zenith.

I said, *'Ta-dah!'*

227

When I went to bow I realized for the first time that Nathan was standing next to me. I gasped. He was wearing the spangly cape. And instead of a wand he was waving the fake cigarette about – the one from the Hey Presto Magic Set.

I said, 'WHAT ARE YOU DOING?'

'Just adding to the magic,' he said, standing right in the middle of the spotlight. 'That's my spotlight by the way.' The fake cigarette was pretty real-looking. If you squeezed it, smoke came drifting out and it glowed at the end as if it was really lit. Half the audience were giggling. The other half were tutting.

'You can't DO that,' I hissed. But he just gave his spangly cape a flourish, and poked at the balloon with the cigarette's glowing end. Everyone jumped back in their seats, expecting the big bang.

The balloon didn't burst.

Of course it didn't.

Because it wasn't a real cigarette.

Everyone cheered and clapped. Except for one person, sitting right behind all the famous magicians. Captain Jimenez! Can you believe it!? So that was her urgent appointment! She had a ticket for the show and never mentioned it.

She wasn't clapping because I could see her reaching for her walkie-talkie.

This was not good.

This is trouble.

Then I looked behind me.

A huge glass wall had been lowered into place across the back of the stage.

And behind the glass, stood the Master of Mystery himself – Perplexion.

CHAPTER FORTY

A DREAM COMES TRUE

NATHAN:

I know Middy says there's no such thing as magic.

But I was right there on stage just a few feet away when Perplexion did the thing he is most famous for – walking through a sheet of glass. He strolled through that glass like it was made of mist. But when he turned round and banged it with his hand, it rang like glass.

Patterns flickered across the glass like lightning bolts.

Perplexion crossed the stage and clicked his fingers at me. Magicians can always tell what other magicians are thinking when they're on stage. Perplexion was thinking – *give me back my spangly cape right now.*

I held it out to him.

He swirled it round his shoulders

Zenith moved to the front of the stage. 'Beautiful people, esteemed magicians and masters of illusion, we thank you for letting us share with you our latest discovery . . .' she pointed at us. We took a bow, expecting her to tell people what we were called. But she didn't know what we were called. So I looked at Middy and she looked at me.

I spread my hands and called out:

'Whoever you are,
Whatever you are,
We have been . . .'

we did the last bit together, '. . . THE WONDER BROTHERS!'

The whole crowd went crazy. Everyone was so pumped.

'And now,' said Zenith, cutting our applause dead. 'Perplexion offers you, his last and greatest illusion.'

The audience held its breath. I swear you could hear their hearts ticking it was so quiet.

Zenith pointed at the big glass screen. The lightning bolts stopped and a picture appeared. A picture of Blackpool, back in the black and white days when the Tower was still towering over the promenade.

'Blackpool,' said Zenith. 'The Home of Magic. Its Tower is a wonder of the world. But then . . .'

There was news footage of people pointing and being sad because the Tower had vanished. Then a clip of us played across the screen.

I shouted, 'Look! That's us!' Everyone laughed. It was the clip of me saying that I was going to get the Tower back.

Zenith shushed the audience. 'The Tower vanished. The sad little town lost its great wonder. The people despaired. But two children travelled . . . Alone . . .'

In the front row, Brodie coughed and said, 'Three actually. I came too.'

But Zenith kept on talking. '. . . Across half the planet to find . . . the only person who could bring that wonder back . . .' She flung her arms wide. The spotlight span across the stage as though she'd thrown it. It landed on Perplexion. His silver trousers dazzled. He looked like a human firework. Zenith said, 'Well I guess you know who I'm talking about.'

Which was true. Of course we knew who she was talking about. But how did HE know about US?

On the other hand, how does Perplexion do anything?

Zenith was still talking to the audience, 'We go live now,' she said, 'to a town without wonder.' The screen grew bigger, like it does in the cinema when the trailers are over and the movie is about to start. Everyone hushed. 'It's early morning in Blackpool. The sun is rising over an empty horizon . . .'

I'll tell you what, it did look bleak. Dark, windy and most of all, Tower-less. I shivered just looking at it. I was so glad to be in nice warm Las Vegas. Middy didn't feel the same. I can always tell what she's thinking. She was thinking – I want to go home.

A clutch of chilly-looking children – all wrapped up against the morning cold – stood shivering and staring sadly into the empty space beyond the security barrier.

One of them held up a copy of today's newspaper to prove to everyone that this was live.

Zenith said, 'Great magicians have vanished big objects before. A grand piano. Mr Copperfield even vanished the Statue of Liberty. An incredible feat.'

The whole audience agreed that that was an incredible feat. David Copperfield gave everyone a little wave.

'But . . .' said Zenith, 'forgive me for saying so, David, but Lady Liberty only vanished for a few minutes. This Tower – fifty metres taller than the statue of Liberty . . . has been missing for *days*. Missing so long that people have begun to forget what it looked like. That's why we have asked some of them to help the Master of Mystery to remember the Tower. To help him see it in his mind before he brings it back into the world.'

One of the chilly-looking children came onto the screen to say that the Tower was tall and mostly made of iron. Another one said, 'It was old, like. Older than my grandad even. Oh. And you had to pay to get in. It looked red in the daytime.'

'No,' said the first kid, 'it looked silver.' They began to bicker about what colour the Tower was. Some of the other kids began to join in. One of them started to cry because he couldn't remember the Tower properly. But Zenith shushed them.

'As you can see,' she said, 'the Tower is already fading from memory. It won't be long before people start claiming there never WAS a Tower. So Perplexion asks that you bring him your memories. Concentrate. Try to see the Tower in your minds. And he will help you bring it to life.'

Perplexion stood with his fingers pressed against his forehead as if he could hear everyone's thoughts. He looked tensed, like he was about to run a race in the Olympics. Oh. Guess what!? His watch was back on his wrist. He'd taken it off my wrist and put it back on.

'Perplexion is thinking,' said Zenith. 'The Master of Mystery is thinking the Tower back into this world.'

I could almost hear the memories myself – all the couples who'd gone there on their first date. The old lady who'd climbed it just to be nearer to heaven. And my own memories too – like shouting, 'I can see it!' as soon as it poked its head over the trees when we were on our way to Middy's.

Perplexion suddenly jumped to his feet. He made a heart shape with his hands and held it high above his head.

His hands glowed red, like a real heart.

He waved his hands apart and blew a kiss.

The red heart flew away from him like a bird set free.

It seemed to land on the screen.

But as we watched we could see it wasn't on the screen at all. It was half a world away, in the middle of the air, hovering over the Prom. And suspended in the air, above Blackpool, the heart began to beat.

Then the magic began.

If you saw it, you'll never forget it.

If you didn't, it's on YouTube.

MIDDY:

That floating heart glowed redder and redder with each beat. And with each beat it got bigger and bigger.

Something was waking up.

The heart thumped. The picture on the screen grew clearer. Lines began to appear in the air, as though an invisible hand was sketching a ladder into the sky.

Then two magical figures appeared from the crowd dressed in golden capes, their hoods pulled over their heads. Between them, they were carrying a box. Mist swirled all around. Maybe it was dry ice smoke. Maybe it was just one of those Blackpool mornings.

Then Perplexion pointed to the ground.

Half a world away, the assistants in golden capes placed the box on the ground. Perplexion then pointed up in the air and, as if they were his puppets, the golden figures lifted the lid of the box.

BANG! The box expanded.

Just like my lunchbox trick.

But faster, much faster, and bigger, much bigger and so, so loud. Their golden capes whirled and shone as they leapt out of its way. Then on the giant screen, the camera pointed skywards. Great iron bones glowed red in the dawn light. And there it was. Blackpool Tower, our Tower, its big heart beating for all of us.

A wonder of the world.

The audience went crazy. David Copperfield actually stood up. One by one all the other great magicians in the world stood up to applaud.

Even though you knew it was impossible, you still sort of believed that the Tower had been hidden away in a little box all this time and now it had jack-in-the-boxed back out of it.

But the trick was not over. Perplexion hushed the audience. Zenith spoke. 'A vanishing trick,' she said, 'reminds us of the joy we feel when we find at last something that we thought was lost forever. The Tower was not all that was lost. These children too were lost, here in Las Vegas. Until now.'

Perplexion pointed at the screen again in Blackpool. The golden caped assistants came right up to the camera. Perplexion waved his hand over his head – the golden hoods swept back, and we saw their faces.

It was Mum.

And Dad.

From five thousand miles away they waved at me.

I didn't know what to say. But I could remember what Karabas said, '*The really magic thing that appears at the end of a vanishing trick is not the wedding ring or the car keys. It's love.*'

Dad knew what to say of course. He said, 'Is Brodie

there? Brodie, you promised to get these two home for tea.'

And for some reason this seemed to be the perfect thing to say. The audience jumped to their feet. Perplexion gestured for me, Nathan, Brodie and Queenie to take a bow with him and Zenith.

Then everything went quiet.

Everyone seemed to know that something amazing was going to happen. Another trick maybe? But what would you do for a finale after you'd un-vanished a five hundred foot tower. This is what Perplexion did . . .

He spoke.

After all these years he finally spoke.

'I vanished a tall building,' he said, 'and that was a trick. But these children crossed the seas, to ask me to bring it back. And that was a wonder.' His voice was like the waves on the sand at night. Sort of, I don't know. Strong and shushed.

'Magicians,' Perplexion said, 'come and go. But the magic must go on.' Then he took off his spangly cape and draped it round Nathan's shoulders. 'Our little lives,' he said, 'are rounded by a sleep. So now, goodnight.'

And then Perplexion lifted his wand in the air and broke it in half. This was a solemn moment. It meant he wouldn't be doing any more magic.

The Master of Mystery bowed for the very last time.

Zenith flicked her eyebrows up at me and nudged me forward. This time I knew exactly what to say. I looked down at the audience.

I said, 'Ta–dah!'

NATHAN:

I wondered what Perplexion would do. How do you leave the stage for the very last time? I looked around and was just in time to see him and Zenith sort of melting into the glass screen. They disappeared right in front of our eyes. Even Middy can't work out how they did that.

The audience kept clapping. I think they thought if they clapped long enough, Perplexion and Zenith would come back for an encore. But they didn't. So we just stood there soaking up their applause.

We were the Wonder Brothers, live on stage, in Las Vegas.

It was literally a dream come true.

CHAPTER FORTY ONE

BROKEN WAND

RADIO LANCASHIRE:

'Today we have good news: Officers from Lancashire Constabulary's Operation Tower have confirmed that the three missing children – Middy, Nathan, and Brodie – are coming home. Along with their rabbit, Queenie. They set out to recover the lost Tower of Blackpool and recover it they did. People from all the four corners of the earth are flocking here, to look up at our Tower, and try to imagine how anyone could have made it disappear. Here in magic's own hometown, we think we already know the answer to that one.

It was magic.

Pure and simple.'

NATHAN:

We never saw Perplexion again. Nobody ever did. He

completely vanished. No one ever even knew his real name. But he sent us back to Blackpool in his private plane! My second time flying. And this time we all had window seats. The pilot kept telling us where we were. So now we can say we've been in Canadian air space and seen bits of Greenland and lots of Atlantic Ocean. Mostly we could only see cloud, piled up like towers and palaces. Staring out across them Brodie suddenly said, 'What happened to all that money we didn't win? Did it vanish?'

'The hotel got a lot of bad publicity for not paying out,' said Zenith. 'So they made a big donation to the nuns.'

We agreed that this was a grand idea and that nuns would do something good with it.

'It'll keep them in Pop Tarts for a while anyway,' said Nathan.

Zenith came with us all the way. She drove us home from the airport in a big fancy hire car.

I called 'Shotgun! Shotgun!' and got to ride in the front seat. So I was the first to spot the Tower – just the tip, sticking up over the roofs and trees. Looking just the way it did every summer when we drove up to stay at Middy's. And just like in the summer I shouted, 'Dibs! First to see it!' and the other two leaned forward in their seat so they could see it too.

I don't think we really believed the Tower was back until then.

Zenith said she absolutely had to come with us

because, 'I need to make sure the whole Tower really is back. Perplexion was worried that maybe one of the legs might still be missing.'

'Not sure,' said Brodie, 'wouldn't it have fallen over if . . .'

Middy pointed out that Zenith was joking. 'What if,' she said, 'you tell us about how you did it?'

'Oh it was easy,' said Brodie, 'a bit of misdirection. I didn't have tickets but I knew the way to the under-stage area. So I handed Queenie to Sergeant Jamie and said she needed a cuddle. Now that's what I call misdirection! While he was cuddling her, I sneaked in and I used the trap door to get up to . . .'

I said, 'Brodie, we're not talking about how you got onto the stage. We're talking about how Perplexion made Blackpool Tower disappear.'

'Oh. Right.'

Zenith said, 'You don't really think I'm going to answer that do you?'

'Sorry. We shouldn't have asked really.'

'That's OK. There might be someone else who can answer.'

As she said that, her phone started buzzing. She put it on speaker. It was Middy's mum.

MIDDY:

'Mum! Dad! We can see it. We can see the Tower.'

'Well,' said Mum, 'We can't.'

'What do you mean?'

'We're in Blackpool,' she said, 'but we can't see the Tower. Think about it. See you soon.'

She hung up.

I said, 'What's happening? Why can't she see the Tower.'

'The thing is,' said Zenith, looking at me in the rear view mirror. 'You're local heroes now. The whole town is excited about seeing the children who brought the Tower back to Blackpool. There's a whole crowd of people from the papers and the TV outside your house. So I'm going to drop you at the only place in Blackpool where you can't see the Tower.'

Brodie asked her how she could put on a show without Perplexion. She said, 'Just because he's stopped doing magic, doesn't mean I have to. I was never just the glamorous assistant. I'm a magician too.'

Nathan said, 'Are you going to be a magician in Las Vegas? Because I could be your glamorous assistant if you like. I wouldn't mind going back to Vegas.'

'Oh. But what would happen to the Wonder Brothers then?'

Nathan said he hadn't thought of that. Zenith

stopped the car outside the Albert and the Lion saying, 'This is where you get off.'

We said our goodbyes. Nathan tried to give Perplexion's cape back to her.

Zenith waved it away. 'Keep it. He wants you to have it,' she said. 'He doesn't need it any more. But the world does. The world always needs a bit of magic. Then she turned to me and said, 'It also needs its lunch,' and she gave me back my Exploding Lunchbox. 'Works a treat,' she said. 'Keep doing it.' She also gave Brodie something – Perplexion's watch! Nathan pointed out that Brodie wasn't a Wonder Brother. Zenith said, 'Without Brodie there's no Queenie. I hate to tell you this, guys, but Queenie's the star of your show.'

Then she gave me something amazing. The two pieces of Perplexion's wand. 'Oh,' I said, 'but that's . . . I can't . . .'

'Is it because it's broken?' she said, passing her hand over the two pieces. 'There,' she smiled. 'All is now restored.' The wand was back in one piece. Zenith winked at me. 'Here,' she said, 'my card.'

She gave us one of those little business cards with her name – Zenith, Queen of Mystery – and her phone number printed on it in a serious-looking font.

'Oh right,' said Nathan. 'And here's ours.' He handed her a Wonder Brothers business card. I didn't even know there was such a thing as a Wonder Brothers business

244

card but it turns out Nathan has pockets full of them.

'Smart move,' laughed Zenith. And she drove away. So we were back where it all started, on the Prom. I looked up.

Of course!

That's where Mum and Dad were. The only place in Blackpool where you couldn't see the Tower.

The top of the Tower.

CHAPTER FORTY TWO

THE WALK OF FAITH!

MIDDY:

Even though we knew the Tower vanishing had been an illusion, it still felt quite scary to climb it. If something has vanished, you can't help feeling it might vanish again. We must have looked nervous because when we climbed the stairs to the Walk of Faith at the very top, Mum was waiting there. She reached down to help us up the last few steps.

'You know,' she said, 'the Tower never really disappeared. People just couldn't see it any more. The wonder is always there. People just lose sight of it. You helped them to see it again. Come here.'

I buried my face in the collar of her coat but all the time I was trying to think where I'd heard those words before.

Dad was talking now, saying how hard it had been to keep the secret of the vanishing Tower. 'Perplexion wanted his world tour to end with something world-beating. And where could be better to do that than here in Blackpool, the home of magic. He needed help to make it work. Assistants. Not glamorous assistants. People who knew all about the Tower. All its secrets and corners. That was us. Me and your Mum. But then you lot went missing too and that was the worst thing that ever happened to us. Though Perplexion said it was the best thing that ever happened to him.

'Perplexion spoke to you!?'

'He texted.'

'We were so relieved when we heard you were in Las Vegas,' said Mum. 'And Perplexion was so happy. Three little kids from Blackpool travelling halfway across the world to ask a magician to bring back the Tower – that's quite a story. And you know, no matter how big it is, a trick is just a trick if it doesn't have a story. It's the story that makes it magic.'

That phrase 'the story makes it magic' reminded me of something too.

But now Nathan was pointing down through the glass floor to the Tower entrance – hundreds of feet below us. 'Look at this crowd,' he said. 'Are they here to see us?!'

They were.

It was the first time an audience had come to see us since that first magic show in our back garden. Up until now we'd mostly been unexpectedly entertaining queues and crowds. But these people had come to see the Wonder Brothers.

We went down to the Grand Entrance and did every trick in the book. The Exploding Lunchbox – with Queenie coming out to take a bow. Cups and Balls. With Queenie coming out to take a bow – AGAIN. I guess Zenith was right. Queenie is the real star.

Everyone loved Cactus in a Balloon too. They loved it so much I said we could do it again. Brodie said he wasn't sure about this. He reminded us that, 'According to Houdini, once is a trick, twice is a lesson.' As you can see, Brodie is not only officially a magician now, he's officially the responsible older cousin magician. But we did it twice anyway.

And then we did it again.

Nathan did that thing where he handed someone our business card and said, 'Oh but you've got two. Can you give one to the person on your left?' And when they did that, said, 'Oh but you've still got two, madam. Can you give one to the person on your right.' And he kept on like that – the volunteer always seeming to have two cards, no matter how many they gave away. So by the end like a hundred people had our business card. Then he said, 'Whoever you are, Whatever you are, if ever you need some Wonder in your life, our phone number's right there on the card!'

We did not need to talk about what we were

going to do for the big finish. We read
each other's minds and went right
back to the beginning and did the old
'Pen-Disappearing-Up-our-Noses
trick'. But for a final flourish Nathan
grabbed Perplexion's wand and
pretended to shove that up his nose
instead. When he spat it out, the
wand hit the floor and turned
into a bunch of flowers. Nathan
made it look like he'd done
this on purpose, but really we
were as surprised as anyone.

But none of that was the
real magic.

CHAPTER FORTY THREE

TA -DAH!!!

MIDDY:

The real magic happened at the top of the Tower.
With Mum.

When the others were heading for the lifts, I
remembered what it was. The thing about *the wonder
always being there*. The way *a trick needs a story to be
really magical*.

'Mum,' I said, 'Have you ever heard of a magician
called Karabas.'

'Karabas the Modest? Second-best magician of all
time? Of course I have. I had her Hey Presto Magic
Set when I was a kid.

That's when I reached into the air and did a little
sleight so that it looked like something had fluttered
into my hand like a bird. The something was a book –
Karabas, My Secrets Revealed. I handed it to her.

'Oh!' she gasped. 'Look at this. Where did you
find it?'

'In the loft.'

She made a little ah sound and starting flicking through the pages.

'So the notes in the margin . . .' I said.

Mum's face was glowing as though its pages were made of candlelight. 'They're mine,' she said. 'I wrote these notes. I was very serious about magic. I was good. A bit like you, Middy.'

'Why did you stop?'

'Honestly plumbing is more magic than magic. Plus, I didn't have enough pockets. Different now. Girls can have as many pockets as they like.' She handed me the book back. 'It's yours now,' she said. 'You went looking for magic all over the world and it was in your own house all the time. The magic is all around you. You just have to wake it up sometimes.'

When Mum said, that she looked younger. Like a little girl. Like someone seeing something for the first time. That's what magic does, I think. It takes you back to the time when everything is new.

The Sun was going down now, over the sea. The shadow of the Tower was long and dark, passing over the roofs and gardens of Blackpool town like a magic wand. The sunset turning them gold as it passed.

All of this is true by the way. Every word. If you don't believe me, go to Blackpool Prom and take a look for yourself. The Tower is back exactly where it always was. And the magic really is everywhere if you just remember to wake it up.

Ta-Dah.

AUTHOR'S NOTE

Whoever you are. Whatever you are. You probably want to know how anyone could make Blackpool Tower disappear. Well . . .

During the illuminations, Mr McNulty – The Illuminator – fixed it for all the lights to go off. And during the confusion he ▬▬▬▬▬▬ ▬▬▬▬▬▬▬▬▬▬▬▬▬▬▬▬▬▬▬▬▬▬ ▬▬▬▬▬▬▬▬▬▬▬▬▬o when the lights came back on everything was the other way round, and they were looking in the wrong place. That explains how the Tower disappeared at night. This was inspired by the way David Copperfield vanished the Statue of Liberty by simply ▬▬▬▬▬▬▬▬▬▬▬▬▬▬▬▬▬ ▬▬▬▬▬▬▬▬▬▬▬▬▬▬▬▬▬▬▬▬▬▬ ▬▬▬▬▬▬▬▬▬▬▬▬▬▬▬▬▬▬▬▬▬ and that's how he did it

The following morning, Mrs McNulty, Aqua Auntie, ▬▬▬▬▬▬▬▬▬▬▬▬▬▬▬▬▬▬▬▬ ▬▬▬▬▬▬▬▬▬▬▬▬▬▬▬▬▬▬▬▬▬▬ ▬▬▬▬▬▬▬▬▬▬▬▬▬▬▬▬▬▬▬▬▬

██████ called 'coloured air'. It was invented by an eccentric engineer called Yannis Alexis Mardas in the 1960s for the military to ████████ ██████████████████████████ ██████████████████████████ ██████████████████████████ ██████████████████████████ ██████████████████. And that's how it was done.

(This section has been censored in order to avoid breaking Rule One of the Rules of Magic.)

When I was wondering how it might be possible to make a big building reappear I was inspired by the great set designer Es Devlin. She creates shows for people like Beyoncé and Adele. Maybe we could get together and make the Blackpool Tower vanish and reappear one day.

Blackpool Tower is a real tower. The Mayor of Blackpool – Sir John Bickerstaffe – saw the Eiffel Tower in 1889. What was good enough for Paris, he said, was good enough for Blackpool. So, like a magician making an old trick new, he decided to give Blackpool a tower of its own. If the Tower really did move to Las Vegas by the way, it would be OK because it's designed to be earthquake proof. In high winds, it

254

sways from side to side. If it ever does fall over, it's built in such a way that it would fall into the sea, and not on the shops and buildings behind. Imagine the splash! There really is a transparent 'Walk of Faith' at the top. They say the glass is strong enough to hold a pair of elephants.

Most of the tricks and magicians mentioned in this book are real. The Cactus in a Balloon trick is my favourite. It was invented by Chris Pilsworth, a lovely person and a great magician. Even though Chris made up that trick himself he allowed me to give all the credit to Middy McNulty and an earthquake. His kindness is magic. Please go and watch his act online or in real life. It's really wonderful.

Considering that magicians are not supposed to tell anyone their secrets, there are a LOT of great books about magic. David Copperfield's *History of Magic* is beautiful and useful. *Magic Is Dead* by Ian Frisch is a great read, as is *Fooling Houdini* by Alex Stone. I really, really recommend Nate Stanniforth's *Here Is Real Magic*.

The heroine of this book is entirely made up but I borrowed her name from a real-life person called Middy McNulty. One Winter's night, our car broke down and Middy appeared out of the shadows to cheer us all up with a bit of magical kindness, like a really cheerful guardian angel. I named my

Middy after her as a thank you.

Also: Muchas gracias a Pilar por corregir mi español!

I started to think about magic when I took my amazing grandson, Patrick Roose, to school one day. He walked quietly up to some friends and stuck his pencil up his nose (by sleight of hand of course!) then he coughed it up again. The whole playground went crazy. Thank you Patrick, you're truly a wonder.

The magician Robbie Danson gave me my first lessons in magic. But more importantly he did some magic for my mum on her birthday. I'll never forget the surprise and delight on her face. She died very suddenly and unexpectedly – like a tower disappearing – just a few weeks later. The magic and the wonder never disappeared though.

The greatest magician I have ever met in my life is my extraordinary editor Sarah Dudman. The great poet Rilke wrote, 'in the kingdom of enchantments our humdrum words are lifted high above'. She lifts my humdrum words to enchantment. And even more amazingly she made an elephant completely disappear over night. Ask anyone. It's true.

Finally all the magic in my life comes from a spell cast long ago with the help of a magic ring by my wife, Denise.

SOME MAGIC WORDS AND PHRASES USED IN THIS BOOK

 Flash Paper –
A special effect. Makes a fiery flash. Very good for getting people's attention, also for misdirecting people's attention (see 'misdirection' below).

 Flourish –
A fancy move to show how good you are at, for instance, shuffling cards. Middy is very much against all flourishes. Nathan is all for flourishes.

 Gimmick –
A false panel or a secret section in any magical object that allows you to hide or produce things. Any trick that you can buy in a magic shop is also called a gimmick.

 (*verb*.) **'to gimmick'**
To secretly adjust an object – say a hat, or a ring or a pack of cards – so you can do magic with it.

 Impromptu –
A trick you can do without any special preparation (like making a pencil vanish up your nose).

Invisible Deck –
A deck of cards that has been gimmicked – usually because one of the cards is back to front.

Invisible Thread –
Super thin string that you can loop around objects and so make it seem like they are floating or levitating.

 Magician's Wax –
A thin clear wax that you rub on things to make them stick to your hands or fingers. Very useful when making things vanish.

 Misdirection –
Making sure the audience is paying attention to the wrong thing so that the trick can go right. Whenever Queenie pops up she misdirects the audience because they can't look away from her wiggly ears and twitchy nose.

 Palm –
Hiding something in your hand.

 Pochette –
Big, hidden pockets that you can hide things in. Back in the day people sewed them into tailcoats. Perplexion's spangly cape is full of pochettes.

 Sleight –
Any secret, hidden move. Sleight is the most important thing to learn in magic.

 Stooge –
Someone who pretends to be just a member of the

audience but is actually in on the trick (this is cheating).

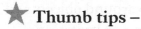

Thumb tips –
A hollow plastic or rubber thumb that fits over your thumb so that you can hide small objects inside it.

Wand –
You know what a wand is. And you know that wands don't really have magic powers. EXCEPT – if you've got a wand in your hand people somehow don't suspect you of hiding something else in your hand. So you can hide a card, a ring, a handkerchief or whatever in your hand if you're holding a wand. Magicians say the wand 'acquits' the hand. Wands and things like wands are sometimes called 'acquittals'.

AND MORE MAGIC WORDS THAT DIDN'T MAKE IT INTO THE STORY – BUT I WISH THEY HAD . . .

Clean –
When, at the end of a trick, your hand really doesn't have anything in it so you can show your hand to the audience. Nathan came up with a way of finishing the Pen up Your Nose trick with clean hands (by pretending to cough up the pen).

Dirty Hands –
When at the end of a trick you're still hiding something

in your hand that you don't want the audience to see. When Middy first did the Pen up Your Nose trick, her hands were dirty at the end.

 Fairy Dust –
Some magicians keep glitter in their pockets and sprinkle it around to 'make the magic happen'. But really it's just an excuse to put your hand in your pocket and hide something in there.

 False Shuffle –
When you make it look like you've shuffled a pack of cards but really the cards haven't moved at all. This is really hard to do.

 French Drop –
A special kind of sleight where you make it look as though you've passed an object from one hand to the other but in reality you've dropped the object into the palm of your hand, to hide it.

 Loading –
Secretly hiding an object somewhere before a show starts so that you can make it appear during the show. The great Malini used to hide things in people's houses WEEKS before he did his trick. Once he even visited a friend's tailor and paid him to sneak a playing card into the lining of his tuxedo so that he could magically 'find' the card there months later.

★ Out (noun.) 'an out' –
A good, clear ending to a trick. Nathan thought that Middy's onions and flowerpots version of the ancient Cups and Balls trick didn't have a good 'out'. In the end it was Queenie who gave them the out.

★ Sleeve (*verb*.) 'to sleeve' –
To hide something up your sleeve.

★ Sphinx Effect –
If you place two big mirrors at right angles in a room covered with patterned wallpaper, the audience won't be able to see the mirrors so you can hide things behind them. Houdini used something like this to make an entire elephant disappear at the Hippodrome in New York in 1918. He fired a pistol into the air and the elephant just vanished! The elephant's name was Jennie and she weighed 10000 lbs.

★ Subtlety –
A way of performing a well-known trick that makes it look more real. For instance doing the Cups and Balls with flowerpots and onions.

★ Talking –
When one of your props makes an unexpected noise that gives the game away, you might say, 'My top hat is talking!'

ABOUT THE AUTHOR

Frank Cottrell-Boyce loves magic. He tries his best with playing cards, rabbits and top hats but is happiest playing around with the magic of words. He's written many award-winning children's books including *Cosmic* and *Noah's Gold*. He's also written films – including *Millions*, and *Kensuke's Kingdom* – and helped create big events like the 2012 Olympics Opening Ceremony.

Frank lives by the sea in Liverpool. On a clear day he can see Blackpool Tower from the end of his road. On cloudy days he worries that it might have disappeared.

ABOUT THE ILLUSTRATOR

Steven Lenton is a multi-award-winning illustrator, originally from Cheshire, now working from his studios in Brighton and London with his dog, Big Eared Bob. He has illustrated many children's books including *How To Grow A Unicorn* by Rachel Morrisroe, *The Taylor Turbochaser* by David Baddiel, *The Hundred And One Dalmatians* adapted by Peter Bently, the Shifty McGifty and Slippery Sam series by Tracey Corderoy and the Sainsbury's Prize-winning The Nothing To See Here Hotel series written by Steven Butler. He has illustrated two World Book Day titles and regularly appears at literary festivals and live events across the UK. Steven has his own Draw-along YouTube channel, showing how to draw a range of his characters. He has also written the multi award-nominated young fiction series Genie and Teeny. For more info visit stevenlenton.com